INFERNO

from
The Divine Comedy by Dante Alighieri

Originally translated by Henry Wadsworth Longfellow

Translated into Modern English by Douglas Neff

CONTENTS

INFERNO: CANTO I

Midway through the journey of my life
I found myself lost in a dark forest,
Having wandered off the main path.

It is hard for me to express in words
How savage, rough, and stern this forest was to me.
The very thought of it renews my fear.

It was so bitter that death could not be worse;
But in order to show you the good that I eventually found,
I must first tell you of the other things I saw.

I cannot remember how I entered the forest,
My thoughts were full of other things
When I wandered off the path.

But then I had reached the foot of a mountain,
At the point where the forest came to an end.
Until that time, I felt lost, and my heart was full of fear.

Then I looked up, and I saw its crest,
Already bathed in the rays of the sun
Which had lead many others to the right path.

Then my fear was calmed a little
And my heart was feeling stronger, having survived
The night, which I had passed so piteously.

And even as a man, who, with labored breathing,
Crawls out of the sea and onto the shore,
Will turn to look back at the perilous water;

My soul, still fleeing from fear,
Turned back to look at the pass

Which no living person had ever left.

After I rested my weary body,
I resumed my journey along the mountain path,
So narrow, that one foot was always lower on the slope.

As soon as I started to climb, I saw
A panther light and swift,
Covered in her spotted skin!

She never moved from my sight,
And many times blocked my way,
So that I had to turn off the path to retreat.

It was still early in the morning,
And the sun was rising, joining the last stars
That were with him in the sky, since time had first begun

When these wondrous things were first set in motion;
So, I took all of these as a sign of good luck.
The variegated skin of that wild beast,

The early morning sun, and the joyous season;
I was able to push my fear aside
Until a lion appeared in front of me.

He seemed as if he would charge at me
With his head uplifted, and his hunger deep.
Even the air on the mountain seemed afraid of him;

Then a she-wolf appeared, that was long and lean.
She seemed to be consumed in her greediness,
That had caused many folks to live in fear!

She made me feel so heavy in my heart,
With the fear that came by just looking at her,
That I relinquished all hope of making it to the top.

And like a man who acquires many things,
But then a time comes when he loses them,
He weeps and becomes despondent over his loss.

This is how I felt while being pressed by this relentless beast,
And, coming towards me, closer and closer, step by step
She moved me backward away from the sun.

I turned and began to run to the bottom of the path,
When suddenly, someone appeared in front of me,
Who seemed hoarse from a long-continued silence.

When I saw him standing alone in the vast desert,
I cried out to him. "Have pity on me, whatever you are,
Spirit or real man!" He answered me:

"What am I?; Once I was a man,
With parents from Lombardy,
They were Mantuans both of them.

I was born in the last days of the reign of Julius,
And lived in Rome under good Augustus,
During the time of false and lying gods.

I was a poet, and I sang of that just
Son of Anchises, who came out from Troy,
After the city of Ilion was burned.

But you, why are you going back to your miserable life?
Why don't you climb to the top of the mountain,
Which holds the source and cause of every great joy?"

"Are you Virgil? That prolific poet
Who has spread a river of speech so broad and wide?"
I blushed and turned away from him.

"Of all the poets great and small,
It was your works I studied most and loved best.
I spent many days exploring your verses!

You are my master, and you are my sage,
You, alone, are the one from whom I took
The beautiful style that now honors me.

See that beast? That is why I turned back;
Please protect me from her, famous Sage,
For she makes my heart race and my blood cold."

"It behooves you to take another road,"
He responded, when he saw how frightened I was,
"If you wish to leave this savage place;

Because this beast, which you fear so much,
Will not allow anyone to pass this way,
And she will harass him, till she destroys him;

She has a nature so ruthless and cruel,
That she never satisfies her greed,
And after eating food is even hungrier than before.

She mates with many animals, and there will be
Many more, until the Hound comes, who will finally
Make her perish in her own pain.

He will not feed on either earth or wealth,
But upon wisdom, and virtue and love;
His nation will be between Feltro and Feltro;

He will be the savior of all of Italy,
On whose account the maid Camilla died,
As did Euryalus, Turnus, Nisus, of their wounds;

Through every city he will hunt her down,
Until he has sent her back to Hell,
The place where envy first let her loose.

Therefore I think it best for you
To follow me, and I will be your guide,
And will lead you through the eternal place,

Where you will hear the desperate cries of woe.
You Will see the inconsolable ancient souls,
Who cry out for a second death;

And you will see those who are content
Within the fire, because they hope to come,
Whenever it may be, to blessed peace;

At that time, if you still want to ascend to Heaven,
A soul, more worthy than me, must take you there;
And I will give you to her when I leave;

You see, the Emperor, who reigns above,
Because I was rebellious to his law,
Will not allow anyone to come to his city through me.

He governs everywhere, but he rules from there;
There is his city and his lofty throne;
And joyous are the ones that he selects!"

And I said to him: "Poet, I beg you,
By that same God whom you never knew,
So that I may escape this woe and worse,

Please take me to that glorious place,
So that I can see the gates of Saint Peter,
And also those whose anguish you have told me of."

He nodded and then moved on, and I followed behind him.

INFERNO: CANTO II

The sun was setting, and the darkened sky
Released the other Earthly animals
From their daily toils; and I alone

Made myself ready to sustain the war,
Both of the way and of the woe,
Which I will, from memory, retrace as best I can.

O Muses, O high genius, now assist me!
O memory, that wrote down what I saw,
Here your accuracy shall be revealed!

And I began: "Poet, who guides me,
Look into my soul, see if it is strong enough,
For the arduous path you place me on.

You once said, that Silvius the parent,
While yet corruptible, went to the world
Of the Immortal, and was there bodily.

But the adversary of all evil
Was courteous to him, knowing who he was
And what would become of him,

This, to thoughtful men, seems fitting for him;
For he was from great Rome, and from her empire
The leaders of the church of Heaven would rule;

Going everywhere, speaking only the truth,
He established the holy place, where
The Popes, the successors of the great Peter, sit.

Upon this journey, which you have written,
Aeneas learned many things that would bring about
Both his victory and the papal throne.

And later came the Chosen Vessel, Paul,
Who brought comfort to that Faith,

Which is the beginning of salvation's way.

But why was I chosen to come, and who allows it?
I am not Aeneas, I am not Paul,
Not I, nor others, think me worthy of it.

Therefore, if I resign myself to come,
I fear that coming may be ill-advised;
You are wise, and know what I am saying."

And as a man, who unwishes what he once wished,
And by new thoughts does his intention change,
So that from his original plan he withdraws,

Such I became, upon that dark hillside,
Because, in thinking, I understood the journey,
Which seemed so simple in the beginning.

"If I understand what you are saying,"
Replied the ghost of Virgil,
"Your soul is filled with cowardice,

So many times a man's thoughts will waver,
That it turns him back from honored paths,
As false sight turns a beast, when he is afraid.

So you can be free from this apprehension,
I'll tell you why I came, and what I heard
At the first moment when I grieved for you.

I was among those who are in limbo,
And a fair, saintly Lady called to me
In such a way, I asked her to command me.

Her eyes where shining brighter than the stars;
And she began to say, gentle and low,
With a voice angelic, in her own language:

'O courteous spirit of Mantua,
Of whose fame still endures in the world,
And shall endure, as long as the world endures;

A friend of mine, but not a fortunate friend,
Is so impeded on the desert slope, that he has
Turned from his path because he is afraid,

And may, I fear, already be so lost,
From what I have heard of him in Heaven,
That I have risen to his aid too late.

Please go now, and with your ornate speech,
Say what he needs to hear for his release,
Assist him please, that I may be consoled.

Beatrice am I, who asks you to go;
I come from Heaven, where I must return;
Love moved me and compelled me to speak.

When I am in the presence of my Lord,
Every time will I praise you to him.'
Then she paused, and thereafter I began:

'O Lady of virtue, through you alone
The human race exceeds all things contained
In heaven and Earth and all places in between.

So grateful am I to obey your commandment,
That if it were already done, it would be too late;
You need not ask me again.

But tell me why you chose to make this journey
Descending down from heaven into this place,
And leaving there, where you so wish to return.'

'Since you have asked, briefly will I tell you,'
She answered me,
'Why am I not afraid to enter here?

One should only be afraid of those things
Which have the power of doing others harm;
For the rest, fear not; because they are not fearful.

God in his mercy has created me
So that your misery affects me not,
Nor any flame assails me of this burning.

The Virgin Mary is in Heaven, and grieves
At this impediment, to which I send you,
Such that the stern rules of Heaven are broken.

In her entreaty she called Saint Lucy, and said,
"Lucy, come. A faithful one now stands in need
Of you, and I would like for you to help him."

Lucy, foe of all that is cruel,
Hastened away, and came to the place
Where I was sitting with the ancient Rachel.

"Beatrice" said she, "As one who praises God,
Why do you not help him, who loved you so,
And who, for you, left the unruly crowd?

Do you not hear the pity of his plight?
Do you not see the death that combats him
Beside that river, which flows only to the desert?"

Never were people in the world so swift
To work their way and to escape their woe,
As I, after such words as these were uttered,

I came down from my blessed seat,
Confident in your dignified discourse,
Which honors you, and those who have listened to it.'

After she had spoken to me,
Weeping, with teary eyes, she turned away;
Whereby she made me swifter in my coming;

And unto you I came, as she desired;
I have delivered you from that wild beast,
Which barred the beautiful mountain's short ascent.

What is it, then? Why do you delay?

Why is such cowardice in your heart?
Why do you not have daring and enthusiasm,

Seeing that so many angelic Ladies
Are caring for you in the court of Heaven,
And so much good awaits you at the end?"

Even as the flowerets, by nocturnal chill,
Bow down and close, but when the sun whitens them,
Uplift themselves all open on their stems;

Such I became with my exhausted strength,
And such courage in my heart there surged,
That I began, like an intrepid person:

"I thank her, who encouraged me,
And you, who have obeyed so soon
The words of truth which she addressed to you!

You have filled my heart with such desire
For the adventure, with those words of yours,
That I have decided to follow you on this journey.

Now go, for we share the same will,
You are the Leader, Lord, and Master now."
Thus said I to him; and when he had moved,

I entered on the deep and savage way.

INFERNO: CANTO III

"Through me, the way is to the suffering city;
Through me, the way is to eternal pain;
Through me, the way among the people lost.

It was Justice that moved my Creator;
Divine Omnipotence created me,
The highest Wisdom and the primal Love.

Before me there were no created things,
Only eternity, and I too, last eternal.
Abandon all hope, ye who enter here!"

These words in somber color I beheld
Written upon the summit of a gate;
I said: "Master, I sense much danger here!"

And he said to me, as one experienced:
"Here all suspicion must be abandoned,
All cowardice must be extinct.

We have come to the place that I told you of,
You will see the miserable people
Who have lost the good of intellect."

And then he laid his hand on mine,
Showing confidence, and I was comforted,
He led me in among the secret things.

There sighs, complaints, and loud laments
Resounded through the darkened, starless air,
Almost immediately, I began to weep.

Languages diverse, horrible dialects,
Accents of anger, words of agony,
Voices high and hoarse, and sounds of pounding flesh,

Made up a tumult that goes whirling on
Forever in that air which is forever black,

Even as sand still flies, though the whirlwind has stopped.

And I, holding my head in horror,
Said: "Master, what is this sound which I hear?
What people are these, which seem by pain so vanquished?"

And he said to me: "This miserable place
Maintains the melancholy souls of those
Who lived without infamy or praise.

They are commingled with that cowardly choir
Of Angels, who were not rebellious,
But nor were they faithful to God.

Because of their disloyalty, Heaven expelled them;
But the endless abyss will not receive them,
Because the damned would glorify them."

I asked: "O Master, what is so grievous
To these, that makes them lament so loud?"
He answered: "I will tell you very briefly.

These no longer have any hope of death;
This blind life of theirs is so debased,
They are envious of every other fate.

The world has no record of their existence;
Heaven's Mercy and Justice both disdain them. But,
Let us not speak of them, look only, and then pass."

And when I looked again, I beheld a banner,
Which, whirling round, ran on so rapidly,
That it seemed as though it never paused;

And after it there came so long a train
Of people, that I never would have believed
That Death could have possibly taken so many.

Among them were some that I recognized,

I looked, and I saw the ghost of him
Who made, through cowardice, the great refusal.

Then I understood, and was certain,
That this was the group of wretches
Hateful to God and to his enemies.

These miscreants, who never were alive,
Were naked, and were stung constantly
By the gadflies and the hornets that were there.

Their faces were covered with blood,
Which, with their tears, commingled at their feet,
And were gathered up by disgusting maggots.

And when I looked beyond them,
I saw people on the bank of a great river;
Then I said: "Master, I would like to know,

Who are those people, and what is it that
Makes them appear so ready to pass over,
As I can see, even in this dim light?"

And he to me: "These things will all be known to you,
As soon as we, ourselves, are standing
Upon that dismal shore of Acheron."

Then with my eyes ashamed and cast downward,
Fearing my words might be irritating to him,
I was silent until we reached the river.

And lo! coming towards us in a boat
An old man, with a head of white hair,
Crying out: "Woe unto you, you depraved souls!

Give up all hope of ever seeing Heaven;
I come to take you to the other shore,
To the eternal darkness of fire and of ice.

And you, standing over there, the living soul,
Get away from these people, who are dead!"

But when he saw that I did not leave, He said:

"By other ways, by other ports, to a different shore,
You shall come for passage, not here;
A lighter vessel is needed to carry you."

And to him, Virgil said: "Hold your anger, Charon;
It is willed by one who has the power to enforce
What they have willed; so question us no further."

At that, there was only silence from the fleecy cheeks
Of the ferryman, though his face was livid,
And his eyes were wheels of flame.

But all those souls who were weary and naked, their
Color changed and they gnashed their teeth together,
As soon as they had heard Virgil's cruel words.

They blasphemed God and cursed their parents,
The human race, the place, the time, the very seed
That made them and of their own birth!

Then, all together, they drew back,
Bitterly weeping, to the accursed shore,
Upon which waits every man who does not fear God.

Charon the demon, with his eyes of flame,
Beckons to them, collects them all together,
And beats with his oar whoever lags behind.

As in the autumn-time the leaves fall off,
First one and then another, till the branch
Surrenders all its spoils to the earth;

In similar fashion did these evil seeds of Adam throw
Themselves from the group, one by one, into the boat
At Charon's signal, as a bird is called to its lure.

So they depart across the dusky wave,
And even before they have landed upon the other side,
Again on this side a new troop assembles.

"My son," The courteous Master said to me,
"All those who perish in the wrath of God
Here meet together out of every land;

And they are ready to pass over the river,
Because celestial Justice spurs them on,
So that their fear is turned into desire.

A good soul never passes this way;
And hence if Charon does complain about you,
You now understand why."

This being finished, suddenly the ground
Trembled so violently, that of that terror
Just remembering it, still bathes me with sweat.

The land of tears gave forth a blast of wind,
And a burst of bright red light,
Which overwhelmed me completely,

And as a man suddenly seized with exhaustion, I fell.

INFERNO: CANTO IV

A heavy clap of thunder resounded through the valley
And startled me from a deep, deep sleep,
Like a person who is forcefully shaken awake;

I looked around with barely rested eyes,
Stood up and surveyed my surroundings,
Trying hard to recognize where I was.

I slowly realized that I was standing on the ledge
Of the valley of great pain and suffering,
Which collects the sounds of the endless laments.

It was obscure, hazy, and limitless,
So that when I attempted to see the bottom
I was not able to make out the shape of anything.

"We will descend now into the blind world,"
Virgil said with uncertainty;
"I will go first, and you will follow me."

And when I saw the hesitation in his face, I said:
"How can I come, if you are afraid? Who will be my
Comfort and settle my fears, if not you?"

And he said to me: "The anguish of the people
Who are down here fills my mind with pity
Which you have wrongly seen as fear.

We must get started now, for we have a long way to go."
Then he went in, and this made me enter as well.
We entered the first circle that surrounds the abyss.

Down there, using only my ears to guide me,
Were not lamentations, but only sighs,
That filled the endless and everlasting air.

And these arose from sorrow, not from torment,
From the massive crowds, that we encountered,

Of men and of women and even children and infants.

To me the Master said: "You have not asked
Who these spirits are, which you now see.
But I will tell you, before we go any farther.

These are the ones who have not sinned; and if they had merit,
It was not enough, because they were not baptized
Which is the gateway to heaven in the faith that you follow;

And those that were born before Christ,
And therefore did not know how to worship God;
It is among these that I too reside. I am from here.

It is this defect, and not from any other guilt,
That we are lost. And our only punishment,
Is that we live on desire alone, but without hope."

Grief seized my heart when I heard this,
Because I knew that some great and worthy people
Were also suspended in that Limbo.

"Tell me, Master, please, tell me,"
I began, wanting to know for certain
That Faith alone can overcome such an error,

"Has there ever been anyone, by his own merit, or by
Another's, who was blessed and allowed to leave?"
And he, who understood my hidden question, replied:

"I had not been here very long,
When I saw Christ himself come down,
Wearing the signs of Heaven as his crown.

First he drew forth the ghost of Adam,
And that of his son Abel, and of Noah,
Of Moses the lawgiver, and the obedient

Patriarch Abraham, and King David,

Israel with his father and his children,
And Rachel, for whose sake he did so much,

And many others as well, and he blessed them;
But I will also tell you, that before these
No human spirits were ever saved."

We stopped moving forward as he spoke,
But the crowd continued passing onward like a forest;
A forest, not of trees, but of thickly-crowded ghosts.

We had not gone very far, and were still on
This side of the summit, when I saw a fire
That cast a bright light in the darkness.

We were still a little distant from it,
But not so far that I could not make out some of
The honorable people who were in that place.

"You, who know so many from every art and science,
Who are those, which appear to have such great honor,
That they stand apart from all the others?"

And he said to me: "The honorable names,
That you have spoken so highly of in your life,
Wins them grace in Heaven, that so favors them here."

In the meantime a voice was heard coming towards us:
"All honor be to the pre-eminent Poet;
His ghost, that was departed, has returned again."

After the voice had ceased and was quiet,
Four mighty ghosts approached us;
Their faces showing neither happiness nor sorrow.

Then my gracious Master said to me:
"He with that sword in his hand,
Who comes before the other three, is their leader.

That one is Homer, the sovereign Poet;
He who comes next is Horace, the satirist;

The third is Ovid, and the last is Lucan.

Because each of these shares the same honor
With me that you heard proclaimed,
They also honor me, as I honor each of them."

And I watched as they gathered together
Leaning towards their lord,
Whose voice, over the others, soars like an eagle.

After they had spoken among themselves,
They turned to me with signs of greeting,
And on seeing this, my Master smiled;

They granted me more than honor, much more,
In that they made me one of their own group;
So that I was the sixth, amid such great minds.

Then we continued walking to the light,
Saying things that were best left unsaid,
And yet saying them all the same.

We came to the foot of a noble castle,
Seven times surrounded with high walls,
And all encompassed by a flowing stream;

We passed over the water as though it were firm ground;
Then passed through seven doors with these Sages;
Finally, we came into a fresh green meadow.

People were there whose eyes were solemn and grave,
They had great authority in their bearing;   they seldom spoke
But and when they did, it was with gentle voices.

Then we went through a wall
Into a lofty and luminous opening,
So that everyone around us was suddenly visible.

There opposite, upon the green meadow,
Were pointed out to me the mighty spirits,

Whom I feel exalted to have seen.

I saw Electra with many companions,
And with her were Hector and Aeneas,
Caesar in full armor with his large, dark eyes;

I saw Camilla and Penthesilea
On the other side, and saw King Latinus,
Who sat with Lavinia his daughter;

I saw Brutus who drove Tarquin forth,
Lucretia, Julia, Marcia, and Cornelia,
And saw standing alone, apart from the others, the Saladin.

When I lifted up my eyes a little,
I saw the great master Aristotle,
Sitting with his philosophic family.

Everyone gazed upon him, and all do him honor.
With him, I saw both Socrates and Plato,
Who stood nearer to him than the others;

Democritus, who said the world was chance,
Diogenes, Anaxagoras, and Thales,
Zeno, Empedocles, and Heraclitus;

I saw the good collector,
Dioscorides; and Orpheus,
Tully and Linus, and moral Seneca,

Euclid, geometrician, and Ptolemy,
Galen, Hippocrates, and Avicenna,
Averroes, who made the great Commentary.

I cannot fully describe all of them,
Because there were so many, that even listing them all
I am certain to miss a few.

Our group of six divides, and we again become two.
My guide leads me away from the others, out from the

Quiet, and to a place where the air seems to tremble;

And we again enter into a place where there is no light.

INFERNO: CANTO V

Then I descended out of the first circle
Down to the second, which was smaller than the first,
But held greater suffering, and louder wailing.

There stood Minos, grotesque and snarling; He examines,
Then judges, the transgressions of each person who enters;
Dispatching the soul by coiling his tail.

I will say that when each evil spirit
Comes before him, it confesses everything to him.
This mighty judge of transgressions

Sees what level in Hell is best fitting for each soul;
And he wraps himself with his tail as many times as is equal
To the level he wishes the soul to be thrust down.

There are always many souls standing before him;
They go, one by one, into the judgment;
They speak, and hear, and then are hurled downward.

"You, there. Why have you come to this place of misery?"
Minos said to me when he saw me,
Stopping his judgments while he spoke,

"Be careful how you enter, and who you trust; Don't let the ease with which you entered deceive you."
And to him, my Guide said: "Why are you shouting?

Do not impede his journey which fate has ordained;
It was willed where there is the power to do
What is willed; and so ask no more questions."

And then the sorrowful voices began to grow more
Audible to me; and I found myself where

The cries were so powerful, they pounded against me.

I came into a place that was completely dark,
Bellowing as the sea does in a storm,
When opposing winds clash on each side.

This hurricane that never rests
Hurtles the spirits onward in its forceful gale;
Whirling them round, beating and smashing them.

When they arrive at the edge of the precipice,
Then come the shrieks, the cries, and the sorrowful wails,
There they blaspheme God and all his power.

I learned that this was the place of punishment
For those who were condemned for their lust, who followed their personal passions instead of reason.

And as the wings of birds drive them forward
In huge flocks in the winter months,
So does that blast always propel these evil spirits;

Left, right, downward, upward, it drives them;
They have no hope of comfort, forever,
Nor of rest, or sleep, or even of lesser pain.

And as the cranes in flight go forth chanting,
Making in the air a long line of themselves,
So I saw coming, uttering lamentations,

Shadows borne onward by the unending wind.
Whereupon said I: "Master, who are those
People, being punished in the black air?"

"The first of those, I believe you know,
Or at least have heard of,"
He said to me, "She is the empress of many languages.

She was so completely absorbed in her sensual vices,
That she made lust a part of her law,

In order to remove the blame from herself.

She is Semiramis, of whom you have read,
She succeeded Ninus, and was his spouse;
She held the land which now the Sultan rules.

Next is Dido, the queen of Carthage, who killed herself for love,
And broke faith with the ashes of Sichaeus;
Then Cleopatra the voluptuous."

Helen I saw, who caused great pain and suffering
For many years; and also the great Achilles,
Who in his last hours, fought for love.

I saw Paris, Tristan; and more than a thousand
Other ghosts he named and pointed out with his finger,
Who died because of their love.

After that, I listened as my Teacher
Named the women of old, and once bold knights.
Pity prevailed, and I was very confused.

And I began: "O Poet, please,
May I speak to those two, who go together,
Who seem so light upon the wind?"

And, he to me: "Wait a moment, when they come
Nearer to us; and then you can ask them yourself
How their love brought them here, and they will come."

As soon as the wind brought them in our direction,
I cried out to them: "Oh weary souls!
Come speak to us, if you can."

As turtle-doves, called onward by desire,
With open and steady wings to their sweet nest,
Fly through the air by their desire alone,

So the two came from the band where Dido is,
Approaching us through the whirling air,

So tender was my call to them.

"Oh living creature gracious and kind,
Who comes to visit us in the swirling air
Though we have stained the world with our blood.

If the King of the Universe was our friend,
We would pray to him to bring you peace,
Since you have had pity on our perverse woe.

Ask us what you would like to know,
And we will gladly tell you,
Since the wind around you is now is silent.

Rimini, the city where I was born, sits
Upon the sea-shore where the Po descends,
With all its streams, and comes to rest.

Love, that will swiftly seize a gentle heart,
Seized this man when he beheld my beauty, which has
Since been taken from me, the manner still offends me.

Love, that exempts no one from being loved,
Seized me with the pleasure of this man so strongly,
That, as you see, it has not left me;

Love has brought us to one death;
But the lowest part of hell, waits for the man who killed
us!" They said these words to us.

As soon as I had heard those tormented souls,
I bowed my face, and held it down so long
Until the Poet said to me:

"What are you thinking?" When I could answer, I began:
"Alas! How many pleasant thoughts, how much desire,
Has brought these two to this sorrowful place!"

Then I turned back to them,
And I began: "Your agonies, Francesca,
Make me sad and drive me to weep.

But tell me, when you had those sweet sighs,
How did you fall victim to your own love?
When did you submit to your own desires?"

And she to me: "There is no greater sorrow
Than to remember a happy time when you are
In misery, and that, your Teacher knows.

But, in order to recognize the earliest root
Of love in us, as you so desire to know,
I will tell you, even as you weep.

One day we were reading for our own pleasure
Of Lancelot, and how Love enthralled him.
We were alone and without any fear of being seen.

So many times our eyes drew together during
That reading, and it made us blush and look away;
But only once did it overcome us.

When as we read of the much-longed-for smile
And being kissed by such a noble lover,
This one, who is now always at my side,

Kissed me full on the mouth, and trembled as he did.
The book, and the writer, brought us to that moment.
But on that day, no farther did we read."

And while the one spirit spoke,
The other one wept, knowing what he had caused,
I began to feel as if I was dying,

And fell, even as a dead body falls.

INFERNO: CANTO VI

When I recovered my consciousness,
Which I had lost in sadness for those two lovers,
I was dazed and confused by my surroundings,

I saw more suffering all around me, anywhere I moved,
Whichever way I turned, and everywhere I looked,
New souls were being tormented.

I was in the third circle, filled with rain,
Falling eternal, cursed, cold, and heavy;
Ever pounding, never easing, never ending.

Huge hail, dirty water, and tainted snow,
Fell in torrents through the murky air;
Grinding the pungent earth where ever it landed.

Cerberus, the cruel and uncouth monster,
With his three heads, each like a dog, was barking
Over the people that were submerged within the muck.

His eyes were red, and his beard was black with slobber,
His belly large, and armed with claws on his hands;
He slashes the spirits, flays, and quarters them.

The tortured spirits howl like dogs;
Lying on one side to try to protect the other;
Then turning again, this mass of wretched sinners.

When Cerberus saw us, the horrible beast,
His mouths opened, and he displayed his tusks;
Every limb on his body twitched and twisted.

And my Guide, with his arms extended,
Picked up handfuls of dirt, and with his fists filled,
He threw it into those cavernous throats.

And as a dog, who is constantly barking,
Then grows quiet as soon as he gnaws his food,

For his entire focus turns to eating,

So it was with the muzzles of the filth-begrimed
Cerberus, the demon, who thunders over the souls
So loud that they wished they were deaf.

We passed across the spirits, buried under
The heavy rain-storm, and we placed our feet
Upon the emptiness that was once their bodies.

They were all lying on the ground,
Except one, who sat up as soon
As he saw us passing before him.

"You, who are conducted through this Hell,"
He said to me, "Remember me, if you can;
Because you were born before I had died."

And I said to him: "The anguish which you have
Perhaps makes you escape my memory,
But I don't think I have ever seen you.

So tell me who you are, that you were put
In so miserable a place, to suffer such punishment.
I may yet see worse places, but none so foul."

And he said to me: "Your city, which is so full of envy
That it overflows on all sides,
Once held a serene life for me as well.

Your people gave me the name Ciacco, the Pig;
And for my sin of gluttony, as you see,
I am forever battered by this rain.

And I am not the only one,
For everyone here suffers the same penalty
For the same sin;" And then he spoke no more.

I answered him: "Ciacco, your wretchedness
Weighs on me so that it almost brings me to tears;
But tell me, if you know, what will happen

To the citizens of Florence, the divided city;
Are there any who are honest and just?
Tell me why so much trouble has come there."

And he said to me: "After the tensions become too great,
There will come the bloodshed; and the old party
Will drive the others out by force.

After that, they will also fall
Within three days, and the other will rise again
Lead by one who now is on the coast.

They will hold their heads high,
Keeping the other under heavy burdens,
No matter how they weep and cry in shame.

There are two just men there, but no one listens to them;
Envy and Arrogance and Avarice
Are the three sparks that have all hearts burning."

Here he ended his tearful speech;
And I said to him: "I wish you would teach me,
And speak to me further.

Farinata and Tegghiaio, were once worthy,
Jacopo Rusticucci, Arrigo, and Mosca,
And others who thought to do good deeds,

Tell me where they are, and what has become of them;
For I would very much like to know
If they have gone to Heaven, or if Hell has taken them."

And he said: "They are among the evil souls;
A different sin drags them down to the bottom;
If you continue to descend, you will see them.

But when you are again in the sweet world,
Please speak of me to others so that I am remembered;
I will say no more, nor answer any more questions."

Then turned his eyes and looked away,
He looked at me again, and then bowed his head;
Then he fell back to the ground like the other blind souls.

And my Guide said to me: "He will not wake up again
Until the Angel's trumpet blows;
And the unforgiving judge arrives,

Each one will find his dismal tomb,
Reassume his flesh and his own figure,
And will hear of their sins echoing through eternity."

So we continued on over the filthy mixture
Of shadows and of rain with slow footsteps,
Talking about the afterlife.

Then I said: "Master, these torments here,
Will they increase after the mighty judgment,
Or will they lessen, or will they remain the same?"

And he said to me: "Remember the lesson you have learned in life,
Which says, that the more perfect a thing is,
The more it feels the pleasure and the pain.

Although those poor and tortured souls
Can never attain true perfection,
Their future holds an even greater pain."

We continued walking around the circle,
Speaking much more, which I will not repeat;
Until we came unto the point where the road descends;

There we found Plutus the enemy of all mankind.

INFERNO: CANTO VII

"Papa Satan, Papa Satan, You are my king!"
Plutus said with his clucking voice;
And my wise Sage, who knows everything,

Said, to encourage me: "Do not be afraid of him,
For he does not possess any power
That would prevent you from going down into this valley."

Then he turned around, faced the great beast,
And said: "Be silent, you accursed wolf;
Consume yourself with your own rage.

There is a reason for this journey into the abyss;
It is willed from on high, and Michael will bring
Vengeance upon those who assault the will of the heavens."

Even as the sails inflated by the wind
Will all fall together when the mast snaps,
So the cruel monster fell to the earth.

Then we descended into the fourth chasm,
Walking still farther along the miserable shore
Which holds all the woe of the world.

Where is God's justice? Who heaps so many
New toils and sufferings upon those that I saw?
And why do our transgressions lead us to such pain?

Like the waves created by Charybdis, the sea monster,
That crash against everything they encounter, so here
the People clashed, confined within their semi-circle.

Here I saw more people than anywhere else,
Some on one side and some on the other, grunting and howling,

Rolling huge stone boulders forward by brute force alone.

They clashed together, and then at the point of impact
Each one turned around, rolling their stone the other way,
Crying, "Why do you hoard?" And, "Why do you squander?"

Thus they returned along the gloomy circle
One group on each side, to the opposite point,
Shouting their shameful cries the entire time.

Then each, when he reached the other end, wheeled about
Through his half-circle to begin another joust;
And I, with great pain in my heart,

Exclaimed: "My Master, now tell me
Who these people are, and if they were clergy,
These with shaven heads." And he said to me:

"All of them were lacking Intellect in the first Life.
Those on the right squandered everything They had without restraint.

You can hear their voices barking loudly
Whenever they reach the two points of the circle,
Where they smash into those with the opposite defect.

They are the clergy, those who have no hair covering
Their heads, and Popes and Cardinals, who hoarded
Everything, sometimes spending nothing at all."

And I said: "My Master, among such great men as these
I ought to recognize at least a few,
Who are infected with these maladies."

And he said to me: "You would think so;
But the life they led to make themselves different
Now makes them all the same.

They will smash into each other, forever; on Judgment day, Those who squandered will have only empty fists. And those who hoarded, will be left with only shaven heads.

It is their hoarding and squandering that has
Put them in this state, and placed them in this scuffle;
They did it themselves and I will speak no more of it.

Now you can see the true folly
Of worldly wealth that is committed to Fortune,
For which the human race has no influence;

For all of the gold that is and ever has been
Can never buy these weary souls a single moment of peace." "Master," I said to him,

"Now tell me also, what do you mean
When you say it is in the hands of Fortune,
That controls all of the wealth of the world?"

And he said to me: "O foolish race of man,
How can you not know of her?
Listen and I will tell you who she is.

He, whose omniscience covers everything,
Created all the heavens, and someone to guide them,
Such that each planet would shine on every other one,

Distributing the light in all places equally;
He did the same with the world's treasures
And ordained a simple mistress as its guide,

So that she might change the treasures
From race to race, from one blood to another,
Beyond any reason of human wisdom.

Therefore one person triumphs, and another
Languishes, based on her judgment,
Which is hidden, like a serpent in the grass.

Your knowledge has no influence on her;
She makes provision, judges, and pursues
Her governance, as the other gods do theirs.

Her changes are always happening, without pause;
Necessity keeps her in constant motion,
As each man takes his turn with her.

And for this, she is often crucified
Even by those who ought to give her praise,
Blaming her for their problems and their pains.

But she does not care, and she does not hear it;
As with many of the primal creatures
She plays her game, and happily she rejoices.

But now we descend into an even greater woe;
We must continue on. It is already getting late
And loitering is forbidden."

We crossed the circle to the other bank,
Near to a fountain that boils, and pours itself
Along a gully that runs out of it.

The water was a deep, dark purple;
And we, walking next to the dirty waves,
Headed downward along an uneven path.

The water creates a dirty marsh, which is called Styx,
When it finally makes its way
Down to the foot of the dark, gray shores.

I stood intent, unable to turn away,
When I saw people covered with mud in that lagoon,
All of them naked and with a look of anger on their faces.

They hit each other, not with just their hands,
But with their heads and with their breasts and their feet,
Tearing each other apart with their teeth.

The good Master said: "Son, you are now seeing
The souls of those who are overcome with anger;
And I will also let you know that

Beneath the water are people who sigh and make the water
Bubble on the surface, as you can see where ever you look.
They are stuck in the mire and they say,

'We were lazy and slothful
When we were in the clean air and bright sun,
Holding within ourselves the sluggish life;

Now we are forever trapped in this murky water.'
They keep gurgling this chant in their throats,
For underwater, they cannot say it aloud."

Thus we circled around the filthy lagoon
Along a great arc between the dry bank and the swamp,
Always seeing those who were trapped in the mire;

Until, at last, we came to the foot of a large tower.

INFERNO: CANTO VIII

I will say that long before
We came to the foot of that high tower,
Our eyes were drawn to the top of it,

That is because we saw two flames flickering there,
And in the distance, a third seemed to answer them.
It was so far away, that we could barely see it.

And, turning to Virgil, I said:
"What is this signal, and what is the answer from
That other fire? And who made each of them?"

And he said to me: "Across the turbulent waves
You should be able to see what is there,
Unless the horrid marshy mist conceals it from you."

A bow never shot an arrow
That sped through the air as fast as
A small boat that was moving in the marsh.

It came towards us, over the water,
Under the guidance of a single pilot,
Who shouted, "You have finally arrived, you wretched soul."

"Phlegyas, Phlegyas, you cry out in vain
This time," my Lord said; "You will not have us
Any longer than it takes to pass through the slough."

Like a man who listens to some great deceit
That has been done to him, and then resents it,
So became Phlegyas, seething in anger.

My Guide descended down into the boat,
And then he made me enter after him,
And only when I entered did the boat feel heavier.

As soon as the Guide and I were safely in,

The ancient boat began its journey, displacing
More water than it had done when it carried others.

While we were running through the dead canal,
A person, covered in slime, rose up from the murky water,
And said, "Who are you that comes here before your time?"

And I said to him: "Although I come, I will not stay;
But who are you that has become so repulsive?"
"You see that I am the one who weeps," He answered.

And I said to him: "With weeping and with wailing,
You cursed spirit, you will remain forever;
Even though you are filthy, I recognize you now."

Then he stretched both of his hands to the boat;
And my wary Master thrust him back,
Saying, "Get away. Go be with the other dogs!"

Then Virgil clasped my neck;
Kissed my forehead, and said: "Pitiful soul,
Blessed is she who bore you in her bosom.

That was an arrogant person in the world;
And there is no memory of him ever doing good;
So likewise here his ghost is furious.

So many are seen as great kings up there,
Who, when they come down here, will be like pigs in mud,
Leaving behind only horrible memories!"

And I said: "Master, it would please me a great deal,
If I could see him dunked deep in this swill,
Before we leave the lake."

And he said to me: "Before we reach the other shore,
Your wish will be granted;
And your desire will be satisfied."

A little after that, I saw a fight
With him by the people of the mire,
And I still praise and thank my God for it.

They were all shouting, "Get Filippo Argenti!"
And that cursed spirit of Florentine turned around and
Began to tear his own flesh with his teeth.

We left him there, and I will say no more about him;
Though I did hear a loud wailing afterward,
I kept my eyes staring forward.

And the good Master said: "Even now, my Son,
We draw near to the city of Dis,
With its savage residents and great walls."

And I said: "I can already see its mosques, Master,
Within the valley, burning bright red,
As if they had just risen from the fire."

And he said to me: "The eternal fire
That kindles inside of them makes them look red,
As you can see in this portion of Hell."

Then we arrived within the massive moats,
That circle that sorrowful city;
The walls appeared to me to be of iron.

We made a large arc around the tower until
We came to rest on the shore. Out pilot then cried out
To us, "Get off the boat. Here is the entrance."

I saw more than a thousand fiendish angels
Sat on the gates, cursing and screaming,
They angrily called down.

"Who is this person who has not known death who dares
To go through the kingdom of the dead?" And my
Master Signaled that he wanted to speak to them
secretly.

Their disdain calmed a little and they called to him,
"You can come, but only alone. He must leave now
Though he boldly entered these dominions.

With his boldness, let him return alone;
Try, if he can; but you will remain here,
You who have escorted him through these dark regions."

I became very concerned
When I heard those accursed words;
For I believed that I would never be able to return.

"O my dear Guide, over and over again
You have brought me here safely, and kept me
From imminent peril each time we faced it,

Do not desert me now" I pleaded,
"And if we cannot go forward,
We can swiftly retrace our steps together."

And that Lord, who had led me here,
Said to me: "Do not worry; because our passage
Cannot be blocked. Heaven has sent us on this journey.

But wait for me here, and take comfort
And remain ever hopeful;
For while we are down here, I will never leave you."

So he stepped forward and abandoned me there.
I stood there, filled with doubt,
For I could not tell if he would be allowed to return.

I could not hear what he proposed to them;
But he did not linger long with them,
Then suddenly, they all fled back into the city.

Those wretched angels slammed the gates,
In my Lord's face, locking him out.
He quickly turned and slowly came back to me.

His eyes were cast down, and he had lost
Of all of his boldness. He sighed and said to me,
"Who are they to deny me entry into this miserable city?"

And then said: "I know I am angry now,
But do not fear, for I will conquer them,
No matter what defense they have planned inside.

This arrogance of theirs is nothing new;
For they used it at a less secret gate, when they tried
To deny Christ entry. And that gate is still open.

It is the gate that we came through, with its inscription;
And, as you see, we are now on this side of that gate,
Passing across the circles of Hell, without escort,

Because Heaven wants this city open to us."

INFERNO: CANTO IX

When I saw my Guide was turning back,
The blood completely drained from my face,
Which made his own color return quickly.

He stopped attentive, like a man listening intently,
Because he could not see very far
Through the black air, and through the heavy fog.

"Still it behooves us to win this fight,"
He began; "Or else. . .No, we were offered help. . .
O how I wish that some would arrive!"

I understood and knew what he had started to say,
Though he quickly tried to cover it up,
But his last words were very different from his first;

Nonetheless, I was afraid of what he said,
Because I finished the sentence in my head,
Perhaps to a worse meaning than he had meant.

"Has anyone ever descended from the first circle
To the bottom of this miserable canyon
In which the primary punishment is having all hope cut off?"

He answered me:
"It is very rare that one of us
Makes the journey upon which we go now.

It is true, I was here once before
Conjured by that heartless witch Erictho,
Who summons back the spirits into their bodies.

Soon after I left my body on the Earth above,
She sent me through these very walls,
To bring a spirit from the circle of Judas;

That is the lowest region and the darkest,

And farthest from the heaven which circles everything.
I know this way very well; therefore be reassured.

This swamp, which carries such a prodigious stench,
Encompasses the city of misery,
That we cannot enter without a fight."

I know that he said more, but I can't remember it;
Because my eyes were drawn
To the high tower with the red-flaming summit,

Where I saw, flying fast and reckless,
The three infernal Furies, stained with blood,
Who had the bodies and mannerisms of women,

Around their waists they wore green hydras;
Small snakes and serpents made up their hair,
Completely entwining their savage temples.

And he, who knew well these handmaids of the Queen
Of Everlasting Lamentation,
Said to me: "There they are, the fierce Furies.

This is Megaera, on the left;
The one weeping on the right is Alecto;
Tisiphone is in the middle;" And then he said nothing.

Each was clawing at her breasts with her nails;
They beat them with their palms, and cried so loud,
That I pressed close unto the Poet out of fear.

"Medusa come, so that we can change him into stone!"
They all shouted looking down; "At this moment, we can
Now avenge ourselves for allowing Theseus to escape!"

"Turn around, and keep your eyes closed shut,
For if the Gorgon, Medusa, does appear, and you see her,
You would never be able to return upward."

This the Master said; and he turned me around
Himself, and not trusting my own hands,

He covered my eyes with his own.

For those of you who are educated, understand the hidden meaning
Of the strange words that follow! Suddenly, across the putrid Waves, a blast of sound shot through the air,

Shaking the ground all around us; it sounded like
A violent wind, clashing like the savage heat,
That attacks a burning forest, and, without restraint,

Rips the branches, beats them down, and carries them away;
Pressing forward, laden with dust, it goes unyielding,
And sends the wild beasts and the shepherds running.

He moved his hands, and said: "Look there,
Along the ancient foam,
There where that smoke is most intense."

Even as frogs when seeing the hostile serpent
Across the water scatter everywhere,
Until each one is safely hidden in the earth.

I saw more than a thousand ruined souls,
Thus fleeing a divine spirit
Who walked across the river Styx.

He fanned the putrid air away from his face,
Waving his left hand often in front of him,
And that was the only effort he made.

I knew that he was sent from Heaven,
And I turned to the Maser; but he raised his hand
So I would be silent, and bow before this spirit.

Ah! How scornful the spirit appeared to be!
He reached the gate, and with a small rod
He opened it, with no resistance.

"You cowards, who were banished from Heaven!"

He began as he stood on that horrid threshold;
"Where is the arrogance that you had before?

Think twice before you defy the commands,
From those who can never be kept out,
And who has the power to increase your pains many times.

What good does it do you to butt against such power?
Cerberus tried, if you remember, and for that
Both his chin and throat were peeled clean of their skin."

Then he returned along the murky road,
And said no word to us, but had the look
Of one who was distracted by other thoughts

Rather than those who were in his presence at this time;
So we walked towards the city,
Confident, now that those holy words were spoken.

We entered without any fight or protest;
And I was curious to see
What sufferings this fortress would hold,

As soon as I was inside, I looked around,
And saw graves and tombs everywhere across a massive plain,
Filled with suffering and distress and terrible torment.

Even as at Arles, where the Rhone grows stagnant,
Even as at Pola near to the Quarnaro,
That shuts in Italy and bathes its borders,

The tombs make the ground jagged and uneven;
This is how it was everywhere along this plain,
Except here, they had a crueller purpose;

The flames between the tombs were scattered,
And burned so intensely hot,
That melted iron could not be hotter.

All of the tombs were uncovered and open,
And from them you could hear dire laments,
So that I knew the wretched souls were being tormented.

And I said: "My Master, Who are those people
Lying in those tombs,
Who scream their miserable cries?"

And he said to me: "Here are the Heretics,
With their disciples of all sects,
And much more than you think is held in those tombs.

Here similar people are buried together;
And the graves burn more or less accordingly."
And then as he turned to the right, we walked

Between the tormented souls and high walls.

INFERNO: CANTO X

We walked along a narrow path
Between the graves and the city wall,
My Master lead and I followed behind.

"You have turned to walk me through these
Ungodly fires," I began,
"Please tell me what I want to know;

The people who are lying in these tombs,
May I see them? The covers are already lifted
And no one is keeping guard."

And he said to me: "They will all be closed up
When they return here on Judgment Day
With the bodies they left in the ground above.

On this side is the cemetery
Of Epicurus with all his followers,
When the body dies, he also kills the soul;

But as for the question you have asked me,
It will be answered for you before we leave,
As will your secret wish, that you have kept from me."

And I said: "Good Leader, I only keep the secret
In my heart so that I don't talk too much,
As you have told me, more than once, not to."

"O Tuscan, who walks through the city of fire
And yet is alive, you speak so beautifully,
Please rest for a while in this place.

Your speech identifies you very clearly as
A native of that noble fatherland,
To which, perhaps, I was too harsh."

This sound suddenly issued forth
From one of the tombs; This brought fear to my heart,

And I pressed a little nearer to my Leader.

And to me he said: "What are you doing? Turn around.
Look, it is Farinata who has risen;
You can see him from the waist up."

I had already fixed my eyes on those of the ghost,
And he rose up erect, showing his face and chest
As though he despised his surroundings.

And with a gentle push of encouragement, my Leader
Thrust me between the tombs towards him,
Exclaiming, "Choose your words well."

As soon as I was at the foot of his tomb
He looked me over, and, as if disdainful,
He asked me, "Who were your ancestors?"
I, while wanting to appear friendly,
Did not conceal it, but revealed it all to him;
He then raised his brows a little.

And he said: "Your family has been bitter enemies
To me, and to my fathers, and my friends;
So that twice I had to send them into hiding."

"If they were banished, they returned on all sides"
I answered him, "The first time and the second;
But they could never get it right."

Then there arose from the same grave,
Uncovered down to his chin, a shadow at his side;
As though he had risen on his knees.

He gazed around me, as if hopeful that he would see
Someone else there with me, but after his
Suspicion was wrong, he began to cry said to me:

"If you are able to go through this blind
Prison, on pure will alone, and still be alive,
Where is my son? And why is he not with you?"

And I said to him: "I did not come by myself;
He who is waiting over there, lead me here,
The one that your son Guido despised."

His language and the mode of his punishment
Made me realize who he was;
So my answer to him was correct.

He suddenly jumped up and cried out:
"What did you say? Is he not still alive?
Does he not still carry the light of life in his eyes?"

When he became aware of my delay in answering,
For I had not answered his question,
He fell, and I did not see him again.

But the other one, who had asked that
I remain, did not change his look at all,
He neither moved his head, nor bent his body.

"And if," He said, picking up where he left off,
"They do not ever get it right,"
He continued, "That hurts me more than this wretched bed.

But fifty times will the glow and flame of
The face of the Lady who reigns here appear,
Before you know how hard it is to get it right;

And when you return to the sweet world above,
Find out why people are so merciless
Against my race in every one of their laws?"

So I said to him: "The slaughter and great carnage
Which have stained the land of Arabia red with blood,
Have caused such merciless laws to be made."

He sighed and shook his head,
"There I was not alone," He said,
"And stood with the others who thought we had a just cause.

But in that group I was alone, because when every one
Else agreed to destroy Florence,
I was the one person who openly defended her."

"Very well. May your family rest in peace,"
I then asked him, "Can you answer me one question,
Which has eluded my rational thinking?

It seems that you can see, if I hear correctly,
Things that will happen before they do,
But you don't know what is happening now."

"We see, like those who have imperfect sight,
The things," He said, "That are far away from us;
Such is our gift from the Sovereign Ruler.

But, when they draw closer, we can no longer see them
And if no one tells us what is happening,
Then we have no idea of what is going on around us.

So you can understand that, being dead,
Our knowledge of the future will stop, at the moment
When the portal of the future is closed."

Then I, as if feeling regretful for asking,
Said: "Now, then, will you tell that fallen one,
That his son is still alive.

And just now, when I did not answer him,
Tell him that I did it because I was thinking
Of the problem you just solved for me."

Now my Master began calling me,
And I eagerly prayed that the spirit
Would tell me who was with him there. He said:

"More than a thousand souls lie with me in this grave;
In here is Frederick the Second,
And the Cardinal, and of the rest I will not speak."

Then he hid himself; and I returned to
The ancient poet, reflecting
On what he had said, which seemed hostile to me.

He moved along; and afterward,
He said to me, "Why are you so distracted?"
And I told him everything that was in my mind.

"Remember the words that were spoken against you,"
The Sage commanded me,
"And listen to this;" And he raised his finger.

"When you are finally standing in the sweet glow
Of her whose beauteous eyes behold all things,
From her you will learn the meaning of you life."

Then he turned around and we walked on;
We left the wall, and went towards the middle,
Along a path that leads into a valley,

Which was filled with a putrid stench.

INFERNO: CANTO XI

We reached the edge of a steep bank
Made by a circle of enormous broken rocks,
And came upon a throng suffering more cruel punishments;

Because of the strong and horrible
Stench being thrust out of the deep abyss,
We stepped back and slid behind the cover

Of a great tomb, where I saw an inscription,
Which said: "Here lies Pope Anastasius,
Whom Phontinus drew off the path of righteousness."

"We need to slow our descent,
So that we may become accustomed to this vile smell
And then we will be able to endure it."

The Master said; and to him I said,
"You will make certain that our time is not wasted;"
And he said: "That is what I was thinking.

My son, inside this circle of rocks," He began to say,
"Are three small circles, each on a different grade,
Like those which we are leaving.

They are packed full of cursed spirits;
You will soon see that for yourself,
But I will tell you why they are here.

Every malice that Heaven hates,
Ends in injury; and as such, gives injury to others,
Either by force or by fraud.

But because fraud is only committed by man,
It displeases God even more; Below us are the lowest of these,
The fraudulent, and greater suffering assails them.

Within the first circle are the Violent;
But since violence comes in three forms,
The punishment is divided into three circles.

Violence To God, to ourselves, and to our neighbors;
Both to them, and their belongings,
And I will explain the difference to you.

If you cause death by violence, and painful wounds,
To your neighbor; you may also destroy his belongings
By arson, or other means;

So homicides, and those who strike with malice,
And those who plunder and destroy, are all in
The first round, but divided into different groups.

Man may be violent to himself
And his own belongings; and therefore in the second
Circle, paying the debt that can never be repaid,

Are suicides and those who deprive themselves,
By gambling away all of their belongings,
And then weep when they should have been happy.

Violence can also be done to the Deity,
By denying him in your heart and blaspheming Him,
And by disdaining Nature and all she has to offer.

And for this reason the smallest round
Stamped with its seal of Sodom and Cahors,
Are those who hate God with all of their hearts.

Fraud, which stings every conscience,
A man may practice on those who trust him,
And on those who do not.

This latter case, it would appear, breaks
Only the bond of love which Nature makes;
Therefore within the second circle you will find

Hypocrisy, flattery, and those who deal in magic,

Falsification, theft, and simony,
Panderers, and seducers, and similar filth.

In the former case, they have forgotten about the love
That Nature gives, and the added bond of man,
Which holds a sacred trust.

Thus in the smallest circle, where the center
Of the Universe is, upon which Dis is seated,
Is where traitors are consumed." And I said:

"My Master, the reasoning is clear enough,
And distinguishes this cavern from the others,
And the people who are in it.

But tell me, those we have seen in the far lagoon,
And those who the wind drives, and those who the rain
Beats down upon, And those who met with bitter words,

Why are they not inside of the red city and
Not punished this way, if God has them in his wrath?
And if he doesn't, then why are they punished at all?"

And he said to me: "Why does your mind wander
To places that it should not?
Or, have I missed what you were trying to say?

Have you no recollection of the words
That are discussed in Ethics?
Of the three things, that Heaven will not abide,

Incontinence, and Malice, and Bestiality?
And how Incontinence offends God less,
And attracts less blame?

If you look at this conclusion,
And then recall those who we saw before, those
That are up above us who are also suffering,

Clearly you will understand why these felons
Are separated, and why Divine Justice

Smites them less forcefully with its hammer."

"Thank you for you have healed my distorted vision.
You have satisfied me, now that you have resolved this.
Because my doubt was worse than my not knowing!

But there is still one question that I have,"
I said, "When you said that usury offends
The Divine Goodness. I don't understand."

"Philosophy," He said, "To he who heeds it,
Notes, and repeats it several times,
That Nature takes her course

From the Divine Intellect, and from its art;
And if you look carefully at Physics,
After very few pages you will find,

That your art, as best it can, also follows
Divine Intellect, as the disciple follows the master;
So in reality, your art is, as it were, God's grandchild.

From these two, if you bring to mind
Genesis at the beginning, it behooves
Men to take control of their life and to advance;

And since the usurer takes a different path,
Nature herself and those who follow her,
Disdain him, for he puts his hope elsewhere.

Now follow, as we must go on,
For the sky is quivering on the horizon,
And the sun will be rising shortly,

And the passage down this bank is ahead of us still."

INFERNO: CANTO XII

The place where we were to descend the bank
Was rocky, and more than that,
It was a scene appalling to behold.

Like the ruins of Trent, caused by a landslide,
Started by either an earthquake,
Or by gradual erosion that suddenly failed,

Where, from the mountain's top,
Down to the shattered rocks below,
A jagged path was formed;

Such was the path that we would have to follow,
And on the border of the broken chasm
A Minotaur blocked our way,

He, who was half man and half cow;
When he saw us, he bit himself,
As one who is consumed by rage.

My Sage shouted to him: "Perhaps
You think that the Duke of Athens has returned,
Who killed you in the world above?

Be gone, beast, for this one does not come
From the false clues of your sister, but he comes
In order to behold your punishments."

As a bull breaks loose at the moment
When he has received the fatal blow,
Who can no longer walk, but staggers here and there,

So the Minotaur behaved as well;
And my guide cried out: "Run to the passage;
While he is still in pain, now is the time to descend."

Down we went over that path
Of jagged stones, which often times moved

Beneath my feet, from the unwanted burden.

Carefully I went; and he said: "You are thinking
Perhaps that this ruin was caused
By that brute which just now I stopped.

I will have you know, the other time
I descended to the lower Hell,
This precipice had not yet fallen down.

But truly, if I am correct, a little
After He came, who took from the city of
Dis, in the lowest circle of Hell, the Grace of God,

The sides of this deep and loathsome valley
Trembled so much, that I thought the Universe was
Overjoyed with happiness, but there are those who think

The world changed into chaos;
And at that moment this ancient rock
Was splintered, both here and elsewhere.

But fix your eyes below; for we draw near
The river of blood, within which boils
Whoever did injury to others by violence."

O blind desire, O insane wrath,
That spurs us onward in our short life,
Then so badly boils us in our eternal life!

I saw a huge boiling moat bent like a bow,
Which encompassed the entire plain,
Just as my Guide had said.

And between this and the embankment's foot,
Centaurs were running in line, armed with arrows,
As in the world they used to follow their prey.

Watching us descend, each one stood still,
And from the squadron three detached themselves,
Armed with bows and arrows;

And from afar one cried: "You, who are coming down the hill,
What torture are you seeking?
Stop and tell us; or I will draw my bow."

My Master said: "We will answer only to
To Chiron, when we reach him,
And I see that you are hasty, as always."

Then he touched me, and said: "This one is Nessus,
Who died for the lovely Dejanira,
And for himself, took his own vengeance.

And the other one there, who's head is bowed,
Is the great Chiron, who brought up Achilles;
That third one is Pholus, who is also wrathful.

Thousands and thousands go around the moat
Shooting with arrows whatever soul emerges
Out of the blood, more than his crime allots."

As we approached near to those monsters;
Chiron took an arrow, and with the notch
Parted his beard in the center.

After he had uncovered his great mouth,
He said to his companions: "Are you aware
That the one in back moves whatever he touches?

Those are not the feet of a dead man."
And my good Guide, who now was at his side,
Where the head and body are joined, replied:

"Indeed he lives, and thus I alone
Can show him the dark valley;
Necessity, and not delight, drives us on.

Someone withdrew from heaven,
Who committed me to this task;
And he is no thief, nor am I a thieving spirit.

But it is by virtue that I am moving
Along this savage passage.
Give us one of your soldiers, to come with us,

And show us where to pass over the river,
And who may carry this one on his back;
For he is not a spirit that can walk on air."

To his right Chiron wheeled about,
And said to Nessus: "You, turn and guide them,
And warn the others, if they meet you."

We, with our faithful escort, moved on
Along the brink of the boiling red river,
Where those who were boiling uttered loud laments.

I saw some people buried up to their eyebrows,
And the great Centaur said: "These are Tyrants,
Who dealt in bloodshed and in pillaging.

Here they lament their pitiless deeds; here
Is Alexander, and fierce Dionysius
Who brought Sicily many sorrowful years.

That head there which has the black hair
Is Azzolin; and the other who is blond,
Is Obizzo of Esti, who, in truth,

Was slain by his own stepson."
Then I turned to the Poet; and he said,
"He will go first, with you, and I will follow."

A little farther on the Centaur stopped
Above a person, who sank as far down as his throat,
But seemed to be rising from the boiling stream.

The centaur pointed to him,
Saying: "He is one, who, in God's house, murdered
The heart that is still honored upon the Thames."

Then I saw people, who lifted their heads
From out of the river, all the way up to their chests;
And I recognized many of these.

Thus more and more the river grew shallower
Of blood, so that only the feet were covered;
And there is where we passed across the moat.

"As you have seen on this side,
The boiling stream diminishes,"
The Centaur said, "I will tell you

That on the other side, it declines more and more
Until it reunites itself at its bed,
Where the tyrants groan.
Justice punishes them, for upon that side, is
Attila, who was a scourge on earth,
And Pyrrhus, and Sextus; and forever pulls

The tears which the boiling brings
Of Rinier da Corneto and Rinier Pazzo,
Who made war upon the highways that they robbed."

Then he turned back, and passed again across the river.

INFERNO: CANTO XIII

Nessus had not reached the other side,
When we found ourselves in a forest,
That was not marked by any path.

There was no green foliage, only grey leaves,
No smooth branches, only gnarled and entangled ones,
No fruit trees, just poisonous thorns.

There is nothing like these tangled thickets,
Nor this dense shrubbery built like savage wild beasts,
In the world above, not even between Cecina and Corneto.

This is where the hideous Harpies make their nests,
Those same creatures who chased the Trojans from Strophades,
With sad announcements of impending doom;

They have broad wings, and human necks and faces, and feet With claws, and their bellies are fat and feathered;
They cry their laments from these horrid trees.

The good Master said: "Before you go any farther,
Know that you are now in the second round,"
He began to say, "And will be, until

You come out on the horrible sand;
Therefore look around, and you will see
Things that will give credence to what I say."

I heard, on all sides, lamentations uttered,
But saw no person who might make them,
So, utterly bewildered, I stood still.

He must have thought that I might think
That the voices coming from those trunks,
Were from people who hid from us;

Therefore the Master said: "If you break off
Some little twig from any of these trees,
The thoughts you now have will be entirely wrong."

Then I stretched out my hand a little,
And plucked a twig off of a great branch;
And the trunk cried, "Why do you mangle me?"

After it had become brown with blood,
It continued its cry: "Why do you break me?
Have you no pity whatsoever?

We were once men, and now we are changed to trees;
Your hand should be more merciful,
Even if we had been the souls of serpents."

Like a burning branch, that is on fire
At one of the ends, while the other drips
And hisses with the wind that is escaping;

So from that splinter came
Both words and blood; startled, I let the twig
Fall, and stood like a man who is suddenly frightened.

"Had he believed sooner, "My Sage answered,
"You wounded soul,
What he read in my verses,

Then he would not have stretched forth his hand;
But the truth is so incredible that it caused me
To allow him to break off the twig, which I now regret.

But tell him who you were, so that he can
Make amends by telling of your fame
In the world above, to which he will return."

And the trunk said: "Your sweet words comfort me,
I cannot be silent; and you should not be angry,
That I now want to converse with you.

I am, Pier Delle Vigne, the one who was keeping the keys

Of Frederick's heart, and I turned them to and fro
So softly in unlocking and in locking,

That I withheld his secrets from most men;
Faithfully, I held the glorious office
To the point were I lost both sleep and my life.

Envy, the courtesan who never turned her adulterous eyes
From the house of Caesar,
Became mankind's undoing and the plague of the courts,

She inflamed all the others against me,
And they, enraged, did so enrage Augustus,
So that my great honors turned into dismal mournings.

My spirit, in disdainful exultation,
Thought that by dying, I would escape disdain,
Though I had always been just, I was unjust to myself,

I swear to you, by the roots of this unwanted wood,
That I never broke faith
With my lord, who was so worthy of great honor;

And so if one of you return to the world,
Let him find comfort in my memory, which is still lying
Prostrate from the blow that envy dealt it."

Then he stopped speaking: "Since he is silent,"
The Poet said to me, "Do not lose this time,
But speak, and question him, if you please."

Then I said to him: "Will you please ask him questions
That you think will satisfy me;
For I cannot, because of the pity that is in my heart."

Therefore he recommenced: "So that he may freely
Do for you what you have asked,
Spirit incarcerate, again please

Tell us in what way your soul became bound

Within these knots; and tell us, if you can,
If, from your group, anyone is ever freed."

Then came breathing from the main trunk,
And that breathing became a voice:
"I will reply to you briefly.

When the exasperated soul abandons
The body that has killed itself,
Minos consigns it to the seventh circle of Hell.

It falls into the forest, and no place
Is chosen for it; but where Fortune hurls it,
There, like a small seed, it germinates.

Up springs a sapling, and then a forest tree;
The Harpies, feeding upon its leaves,
Do create pain, and for the pain there is no outlet.

Like others, our souls will return to our bodies;
But not any one of us may wear those bodies again,
For it is not possible to have what you taken from
yourself.

We will drag our bodies here, and all along this dismal
Forest our bodies will be suspended,
By the thorns of our molested souls."

We were still watching the trunk,
Thinking that it might wish to tell us more,
When we were overtaken by a rushing noise,

In the same way one senses
The boar approaching where he stands,
By hearing the crashing of the beasts and branches;

Suddenly, on our left side, naked and scratched,
Fleeing so furiously, Two shapes broke through
The forest, breaking every branch they touched.

The one in the lead said: "Help, Death, help!"

And the other one, who seemed to lag behind,
Was shouting: "Lano, those legs of yours were not so nimble

At the jousting tournament of Toppo!"
And then, because his breath was failing,
He wrapped his arms around a bush.

Behind them was a forest full of black
She-wolves, ravenous, and fast
Like greyhounds, who are released from the chain.

They set their teeth into the one who was crouching,
And they tore him apart, piece by piece,
Taking away his mangled body parts.

Then my Escort took me by the hand,
And led me to the bush, that
Was weeping from its bloody lacerations.
"O Jacopo," It said, "Of Saint Andrea,
What good did it do you to cling to me?
Why do you blame me for your evil life?"

When the Master stopped near him,
He said: "Who were you, that through so many wounds
You are still giving your grieving speech?"

And he said to us: "O souls, that have come
To look upon this shameful massacre
That has torn away my leaves,

Gather them up, and place them beneath the dismal bush;
I was from the city which took the Baptist
In exchange for Mars, its first patron.

For this, his image in art will forever bring sadness.
And were it not for a piece of his statue
Which still remains on the Arno bridge,

Those citizens, who afterwards rebuilt it

On the ashes left by Attila,
Would have done all of their labor in vain.

And, as for me, in my own house, I hung myself."

INFERNO: CANTO XIV

Because my native land taught me charity
I gathered the scattered leaves,
And gave them back to him.   But he was now hoarse.

Then we came to the edge of the forest, where
The second round is separated from the third, and where
A horrible form of Justice is seen.

I will try to explain what I saw.
As I said, we stood at the edge of a plain,
Which rejected the roots of every plant;

The miserable forest surrounded it
All around, as the sad moat surrounded the forest;
There close to the edge we stopped.

The soil was made up of an arid and thick sand,
Much the same as that
Which the feet of Cato once pressed down.

O Vengeance of God, How much
Everyone who reads this should dread
That which was revealed to my eyes!

I saw herds of naked souls,
Who were all weeping miserably,
And each group had a different penalty.

Some of them were lying on the ground;
And some were sitting all drawn up together,
And others walked continually, never stopping.

Those who were going around were far greater in number,
And those who lay down in their torment were far less,
But they lamented more than the others.

And falling over all the sandy wasteland,

Huge flakes of fire rained down,
Like the snow on a mountain with no wind.

As Alexander saw,
In those parched lands of India,
Flames fell unbroken till they reached the ground.

He tried with his armies
To trample down the soil, because the flame was
Better extinguished before it joined with others;

In the same manner, the eternal heat descended,
And the sand was set on fire, like wood shavings
Under metal sparks, which doubled their pain.

Forever, without rest, the dance
Of miserable hands, first here, then there,
Brushed away the falling snow of flame.
"Master," I began, "You, who overcomes
All things except the worst demons, that fought
Against us at the entrance of the gate,

Who is that mighty one who seems not to feel
The fire, and lies there sullen and disdainful,
As though the rain does not burn him?"

And the man himself, who had become aware that I was
Questioning my Guide about him, cried: "As I was when
I was Living, I am the same now that I am dead.

Jupiter will wear out his blacksmith, from whom
He angrily seized the sharp thunderbolt,
That he hurled at me on my final day,

And he wearied out, one by one, the others
In Mongibello at that blackened forge,
Crying out, 'Help, Vulcan, help!'

Even as he did at the fight of Phlegra,
And shot his bolts at me with all his might,
I will not give him joyous vengeance here."

Then my Leader spoke with such great force,
That I had never heard him speak so loud:
"O Capaneus, I see that it has not extinguished

Your arrogance, you are punished all the more;
There is no punishment, except your own rage,
Which could punish you more completely."

Then he turned to me saying in a softer tone,
"He was one of the Seven Kings
Who besieged Thebes, and held, and still seems to hold

God in disdain, and he prizes very little;
But, as I said to him, his own spite
Is his worst punishment.

Now follow me, and mind you do not place
Your feet upon the burning sand,
But always keep them close to the woods."

Speaking not a word, we came to where a little rivulet
Gushes from the woods, and the redness of its color
Makes my hair still stand on end.

As the brooklet springs from the Bulicame,
Which sinful women share downstream,
So the water made its way through the sand.

The river's bed, and both sloping banks,
Were made of stone, as were the edges on each side;
Then I understood that this was our passage.

"In all the things which I have shown you
Since we entered through the gate
Whose threshold no one is denied,

You have not seen anything that is
As notable as this river before us,
Which quenches all the flames above it."

My Leader said; and I asked him
If he would tell me more,
For he had given me the desire to learn.

"In the mid-sea there sits a wasted land,"
He said, "Whose name is Crete,
Under whose king the world of old was chaste.

There is a mountain there, that once was full
With waters and with plants, which was called Ida;
Now it is deserted, as a thing that is worn out.

Rhea once chose it for the faithful cradle
For her own son; and to better conceal him,
Whenever he cried, she had her servants cry out as well.

An old man stands erect on the mountain,
And he holds his shoulders turned towards Damietta,
And looks at Rome as if it were his mirror.

His head is fashioned of refined gold,
And of pure silver are his arms and breast;
Then his body is brass as far down as his hips.

From that point downward everything is iron,
Except for the right foot which is kiln-baked clay,
And he stands on that foot more than on the other.

Each part, except the gold, is broken by a fissure
That is dripping with tears,
Which gather together to erode that cavern.

From rock to rock the tears fall into this valley;
And they form Acheron, Styx, and Phlegethon;
Then go downward along this narrow canal.

At the point where it can no longer descend,
They form Cocytus; and what that pool becomes
You will soon see, so I won't tell you now."

And I said to him: "If the current stream

First begins in our world,
Why does it only appear to us here?"

And he said to me: "You know this place is round,
And notwithstanding you have journeyed far,
Staying to the left, descending to the bottom,

You have not yet gone through all the circle.
Therefore if something new appears to us,
You should not be surprised to see it."

And I said: "Master, where will we find
Lethe and Phlegethon, you have said nothing of them,
But you say that this one is made from tears?"

"It pleases me that you ask so many questions,"
He replied; "but the boiling of the red
Water might well solve one of your questions.

You will see Lethe, but outside this moat,
There where the souls go to wash themselves,
When they have repented and their sin has been
removed."

Then he said: "It is time now to abandon
The woods; take heed that you come after me;
The river border makes a way that is not burning,

And along this path, the flames are extinguished."

INFERNO: CANTO XV

Walking along the stone embankment,
The brooklet's mist overshadows us,
But it saves both the water and the dikes from fire.

As the Flemings, between Wissant and Bruges,
Fearing the flood that hurls itself towards them,
Build their dikes to keep the flood waters back;

And as the Paduans along the Brenta,
Protect their villas and their Castles,
Before Chiarentana feels the heat;

In similar fashion these walls had been made,
Albeit not so lofty nor so thick,
Whoever he might be, the master made them.

Now we were far away from the forest,
I could not see where it was,
Even when I looked behind me,

When we encountered a company of souls,
Who came beside the dike, and every one
Gazed at us, as in the evening we were

To look at each other under a new moon,
And so they came toward us, looking intently
As an old tailor looks at the needle's eye.

Thus scrutinized by such a group,
I was recognized someone, who seized
My garment's hem, and cried out,

"What a marvel!" and I, when he stretched forth
His arm to me, fastened my eyes on his baked features,
Even his scorched body did not prevent

Me from recognizing him;
And bowing my face towards his,

I replied, "Are you here, Ser Brunetto?"

And he said: "I hope it does not displease you, my son,
To share some time with Brunetto Latini
While the rest of the group moves on."

I said to him: "I would enjoy that very much;
And if you wish me to sit down with you,
I will, if my Master does not mind, for I go with him."

"O son," He said, "When someone from this herd
Stops for a moment, he lies there for a hundred years,
Not even fanning himself when he is hit with fire.

Therefore go on; I will follow you from the edge,
And afterward will I rejoin my band,
Which goes on lamenting its eternal doom."
I did not dare come off the road
To walk with him; but I kept my head bowed
As someone who walks reverently.

And he began: "What fortune or what fate
Leads you down here before your time?
And who is this that shows you the way?"

"Up there above us in the serene life,"
I answered him, "I was lost in a valley,
While I was still alive.

But yesterday I turned my back on it;
This one appeared to me, promised to return me there,
And leads me homeward along this road."

And he said to me: "If you follow your star,
You cannot fail to reach a glorious port,
If I judged your beautiful life correctly.

And if I had not died so prematurely,
Seeing how favorable Heaven is to you,
I would have given you comfort in your work.

But that ungrateful and malignant people,
Who descended from Fesole,
And still smell of mountain and granite,

Will make themselves your enemy, because of your good deeds,
And it is right; for among bitter weeds
It does not benefit the sweet fig to bear fruit.

Old rumor in the world proclaims them blind;
A people avaricious, envious, proud;
Take heed that you cleanse yourself of their customs.

You do deserve so much honor,
One party or the other shall be hungry
For you; but the grass will be far from those goats.

Let their litter of beasts from Fesole
Make for themselves, and do not let them touch the plant,
If any should arise upon their dunghill,

In which may yet revive the consecrated
Seed of those Romans, who remained there when
It became the nest of such great malice."

"If my wishes were wholly fulfilled,"
I replied to him, "You would not be
In banishment and placed far away from human kindness;

For my mind is fixed, and it fills
My heart with the dear and good paternal image
Of you, when in the world from hour to hour

You taught me how a man becomes eternal;
And how much I am grateful, while I live
I will always speak highly of you.

What you tell me of my career, I will write,
And keep it to be combined with other text

By a Lady who can do it, if I reach her.

This much will I have promise you;
Provided that my conscience does not chide me,
I am ready for whatsoever Fortune should befall me.

Such prophesy is not new to my ears;
Therefore let Fortune turn her wheel around
As it may please her, as a worker with his shovel."

My Master turned to look over his right shoulder
And gazed back at me,
Then said: "He listens well he who notes all that he hears."

Not speaking less on that account, I go
With Brunetto, and I ask who are
His most known and most eminent companions.

And he said to me: "To know of some is well;
Of others it is better to be silent,
For there is not enough time for so much speech.

Know them in total, that all of them were clerks,
And men of great letters and of great fame,
In the world tainted with the same sin.

Priscian goes yonder with that wretched crowd,
And Francis of Accorso; and you would have seen them
If you had a hankering for such filth,

That one, who is the Servant of the Servants
From Arno was transferred to Bacchiglione,
Where he left his sin-excited nerves.

I would say more, but coming and talking
Must come to an end; for I see
New smoke rising from the sand.

People are coming with whom I must not be;
I give to you my Tesoro, so tell my story,

That I may still live, and I will ask no more."

Then he turned around, and seemed to be like those
Who in Verona run for the Green Mantle
Across the plain; and seemed to be

The one who wins, and not the one who loses.

INFERNO: CANTO XVI

I could hear the reverberation
Of water falling into the next circle,
Like the humming of bee hives,

When three spirits came towards us,
Running, from out of a company that passed
Beneath the flaming rain of bitter suffering.

As they came near us, each one cried out:
"Stop, you; we can tell from your garments
That you are from our depraved city."

Ah me! I saw multiple wounds upon their limbs,
Recent and ancient that the flames had burnt in!
It pains me still to remember it.

My Teacher paused attentive to their cries;
He turned his face towards me, and said
"Now wait," he said; "We should be courteous to these.

And if it were not for the fire that darts
The ground of this region, I should say
That you would be running to greet them."

As soon as we stood still, they repeated
Their refrain, and when they overtook us,
All three of them circled around us.

As champions stripped and oiled will sometimes do,
Watching for their advantage and their hold,
Before they come to blows and thrusts between them,

Thus, wheeling round, every one of them
Directed his gaze to me, so that in the opposite
Direction his neck and feet made a continual journey.

And one said, "If the misery of this soft place
Brings disdain to ourselves and our requests,"

He began, "With our bodies black and blistered,

Let the renown we had when we were alive guide you
To tell us who you are, that you can safely,
With living feet, move along through Hell.

He in whose footprints you see me treading,
Naked and skinless though he may be now,
Was of a greater rank than you think;

He was the grandson of the good Gualdrada;
His name was Guidoguerra, and in life
He did much with his wisdom and his sword.

The other, who stands close by me in the sand,
Is Tegghiaio Aldobrandi, whose fame
Should be well known there in the world above.

And I, who has crossed with them,
Was known as Jacopo Rusticucci; and truly
My savage wife, more than anything else, drove me here."

If I could have been protected from the fire,
I would have thrown myself among them,
And I think my Teacher would have allowed it;

But as I would have burned and baked myself,
My terror was greater than my desire,
Though I wanted to embrace them.

I began: "Sorrow and not disdain
For your condition has fixed me in this position,
And I will remember it for many years,

The moment that my Lord said to me
Words that lead me to believe
That people such as you were approaching.

I am from your city; and for evermore
Your labors and your honorable names

I have heard and repeated with affection.

I leave the bitter, and go for the sweet fruits
Promised to me by my veracious Leader;
But first, I must plunge to the center."

"May your soul live for a long time to conduct
Those limbs of yours," He answered,
"And may your renown shine after you,

So valor and courtesy, still dwell
Within our city, as they used to do,
Or are they wholly gone out of it;

For Guglielmo Borsier, who is in torment
With us, and goes there with his comrades,
Does mortify us with his words."

"The new inhabitants and the sudden wealth,
Have engendered the city with Pride and extravagance,
So you may weep for Florence very soon!"

I exclaimed with my head facing up;
And the three, thinking that was my reply,
Looked at each other, as if it were the truth.

"If you always answer so easily," they all replied,
"To satisfy another,
You are happy indeed, thus speaking as you will!

Therefore, if you escape from these dark places,
And come to see the beauteous stars again,
When it should please you to say, 'I was there,'

See that you speak of us kindly to the people."
Then they separated, and in their flight
It seemed as if their agile legs were wings.

Not an Amen could possibly have been said
As rapidly as they had disappeared;
Then the Master deemed it best to depart.

I followed him, and we had not gone very far,
Before the sound of water was near us,
So that if we spoke, we would hardly have been heard.

Even as that stream which holds its own course
First from Monte Veso towards the East,
Upon the left-hand slope of Apennine,

Which is above called Acquacheta, before
It descends down into its low bed,
And at Forli no longer has that name,

It reverberates there above San Benedetto
From the Alps, by falling at a single leap,
Where there is room enough for a thousand;

Thus falling from a precipitate bank,
We found that dark-tinted water resounding,
So that it soon was deafening to hear.

I had a belt around about my waist,
And with it, I had hoped
To take the panther with the painted skin.

After I had unloosed it from around me,
As my Conductor had commanded,
I passed it to him, gathered up and coiled,

He turned himself to the right,
And very close to the edge,
He cast it down into that deep abyss.

"I know something strange is about to happen,"
I said to myself, "For this new signal
The Master is following with his eyes."

Ah my! How very cautious men should be
With those who do not behold the act alone,
But with their wisdom look into the thoughts of others!

He said to me: "Soon there will come
What I am waiting for; and what your thought is dreaming
Will soon reveal itself to you."

That truth which has the face of falsehood,
A man should close his lips as tight as he can,
Because it causes shame through no fault of his own;

But here I cannot; and, Reader, by the notes
That I have taken to you I swear,
So that they may be received with lasting favor,

Through that dense and darksome atmosphere
I saw a figure swimming upward through the air,
A thing that would shake the most steadfast heart,

Even as one returns who goes down
Sometimes to clear an anchor, which has grappled
A reef, or something else in the sea that is hidden,

Reaching with his arms, and pushing with his legs.

INFERNO: CANTO XVII

"Behold the monster with the pointed tail,
Who cleaves the hills, and breaks walls and weapons,
Behold him who infects all the world."

My Guide began to say,
And called to him to come to shore,
Near to the broken marble bank;

And that unclean image of deceit
Came and thrust up its head and chest,
But it did not drag its tail out of the water.

The face was the fair face of a just man,
Outwardly, it looked so benign,
But it had the body of a serpent.

It had two paws, hairy unto the armpits;
The back, and breast, and on both sides it had
Tattoos of nooses and of shields.

Never were there so many colors, in thread or broidery
In cloth of Tartars nor Turks,
Nor were such tissues by Arachne laid, than on this creature.

As sometimes fishing boats lie upon the shore,
Where part are in the water, part on land;
And as among drunken men laying there,

And as the beaver plants himself to wage his war;
So that vile monster lay upon the shore,
Which is of stone, and keeps out the sand.

His tail was completely covered in spikes,
Holding up the venomous fork,
Like that of a scorpion armed at its point.

The Guide said: "Now we must turn aside

Our way a little, because of that beast
That lies in wait for us."

We therefore descended on the right,
And made ten steps on the outer edge,
Trying to avoid the sand and the flame;

And after we came up to him, I saw
A little farther off upon the sand
People sitting near the edge of the abyss.

Then the Master said to me: "So that you have the full
Experience of this round to take with you,
Go and see what has brought them to this place.

With them, be concise in your conversation;
Until you return, I will speak with the creature,
So that he will carry us on his stalwart shoulders."
Thus farther along the outermost
Edge of that seventh circle
I went all alone to where the melancholy folk sat.

Their woe gushed from their eyes;
Their hands brushed this way and that way,
First from the flames and then from the hot soil.

As in summer the dogs scratch,
First with the foot, then with the muzzle, when
They are bitten by fleas, or flies, or gadflies.

When I looked into their faces,
On whom the merciless fire is falling,
I did not recognize any of them; but I saw

That from the neck of each of them, there hung a pouch,
Which had a specific color, and a coat of arms;
And it was there that their eyes were fixed.

And as I gazed around me and came among them,
Upon a yellow pouch I saw one
That had the face and body of a blue lion.

Proceeding then, I continued to look around,
And I saw another of them, a pouch red as blood,
Displaying a goose more white than butter.

And one, who with a blue pig engraved
In his little pouch of white,
Said to me: "What are you doing in this moat?

Get out of here; and since you are still alive,
Know that a neighbor of mine, Vitaliano,
Will have his seat here on my left-hand side.

I am the only Paduan among these Florentines;
Many times they scream in my ears,
Exclaiming, 'Send down the sovereign knight,

He will bring the satchel with three goats;'"
Then he twisted his mouth, and he thrust forth
His tongue, like to an ox that licks its nose.

And fearing that my staying longer might upset
He who had warned me not to stay long,
I turned away from those weary souls.

I found my Guide, who had already mounted
The back of that wild animal,
And he said to me: "Now be both strong and bold.

We descend by a different kind of stairway;
You mount in front, for I will be here in the middle,
So that the tail will not be able to harm you."

As someone who is near his time in quarantine
Such that his nails are blue already,
And he trembles all over just looking at a shady spot;

That is how I became when I heard those words;
But his stare brought shame into my heart,
Which made me want to look strong before my good
master.

I seated myself upon those monstrous shoulders;
I wanted to say, and could not speak
What I thought, "Please hold on to me."

But he, who had at other times rescued me
In other peril, as soon as I had mounted,
He encircled and restrained me with his arms,

And said: "Now, Geryon, get moving;
The circle is large, and the descent will be small;
Think of the novel burden which you now carry."

Even as the little vessel shoves from shore,
Backward, still backward, so he withdrew;
And when he felt himself afloat in the air,

There where his breast had been he turned his tail,
And with that extended like an eel he moved,
And using his paws he drew himself into the air.

I do not think there was a greater fear
Even the time when Phaeton abandoned the reins,
And scorched the heavens;

Nor when the wretched Icarus
Felt his flanks stripped of feathers by the melting wax,
His father crying, "You are going the wrong way!"

So was my own fear, when I perceived myself
On all sides in the air, and could see nothing but
The monster I was riding.

Onward he went, swimming slowly, soaring easily;
Wheeling and descending, but I only perceived it
By the wind on my face and the open air below me.

I heard on the right of the whirlpool, something
Making a horrible crashing under us;
So I thrust out my head with eyes cast downward.

Then I was even more fearful of the abyss;
Because I saw fires, and heard laments,
Trembling, I clung all the closer.

I saw then, as I had not seen before,
The great horrors that, by turning and descending,
Were closing in on all sides.

As a falcon who has long been on the wing,
Who, without seeing either lure or bird,
Makes the falconer say, "Why is he stopping?"

Descends weary, though he started swiftly,
Through a hundred circles, and dives
Far from his master, sullen and disdainful;

This is how Geryon placed us on the bottom,
Close to the base of the rough-hewn rock,
And once relieved of his load,

He sped away as an arrow from a string.

INFERNO: CANTO XVIII

There is a place in Hell called Malebolge,
Made completely of stone and it has an iron color,
As do the walls that encircle it.

Right in the middle of the horrible field
There is a huge well exceedingly wide and deep,
I will tell you now how the place is structured.

The enclosure which remains
Between the well and foot of the high, hard bank,
Is round and has ten distinct valleys in its bottom.

As if for the protection of the walls
Many, many moats surround the castles,
Together, they form an odd figure,

And that is the image presented there;
Stretching out from the gates of each of the strongholds
Across to the outer bank are little bridges,

At the precipice of each base there are crags in the
Project, with intersecting dikes and moats,
Until reaching the well that truncates and collects them.

We found ourselves within this place,
When we descended off the back off Geryon; and the
Poet
Held to the left, and I followed behind him.

On my right, I saw new anguish,
New torments, and new wielders of the lash,
Which crowded the first circle.

Down at the bottom, the sinners were naked;
On this side of the middle, they faced us,
Beyond it, they faced away from us, but with greater
steps;

As the Romans, when they played the mighty host,
Upon the bridge, the year of Jubilee,
Had to build a way for the people to pass;

So all on one side moved towards the Castle
All facing the same direction, and go to St. Peter's;
On the other side they go towards the Mountain.

This side and that, along the horrid stone
I saw horned demons with the great masses,
Who cruelly were beating them from behind.

Ah me! How they made them lift their legs
At the first blows! And not any one paused
To wait for the second blow, nor for the third.

While I was going on, my eyes
Fell upon one of them; and I said:
"I think I know that one."

Therefore I stopped to make him out,
And with me the Guide came to stand,
And waited to see if I would go back;

And he, the scourged one, tried to hide himself,
Lowering his face, but little did it help him;
For I said: "You who cast down your eyes,

Unless you look exactly like someone else,
You are Venedico Caccianimico;
But what brought you to such pungent waters?"

And he said to me: "I would rather not say;
But your words have forced me to,
For they make me remember the ancient world.

I was the one who the fair Ghisola
Induced to grant the wishes of the Marquis,
However the shameless story may be told.

But I am not the only Bolognese who weeps here;

No, this place is so full of them,
That there are not so many ways taught today

To say 'sipa' between Reno and Savena;
And if you want a pledge or proof,
You have only to remember that we have avaricious hearts."

While he was speaking to me, a demon hit him with his whip, And said: "Get away from here
You pimp, there are no women here for sell."

I collected myself together and joined my Escort;
After a short distance, we came
To where a crag projected from the bank.

Thus very easily we ascended,
And turning to the right along its ridge,
We departed from those eternal circles.

When we reached to point where it is hollowed out
Beneath, to give passage to the scourged,
The Guide said: "Stop and look and you will see

The vision of those others who were evil-born,
Of whom you have not yet seen,
Because they left when we did."

From the old bridge we looked upon the train
Which came towards us from the other border,
And whom the whips struck a like manner.

And the good Master, without my asking,
Said to me: "See that tall one who is coming,
And seems not to shed a tear though he is in pain;

Still what a royal posture he retains!
That is Jason, who by his heart and cunning
Took the ram of Colchians.
He passed by the isle of Lemnos
After the daring and pitiless women

Had all of their males put to death.

There with his gifts and with ornate words
He deceived Hypsipyle, the maiden
Who first, herself, had deceived all the rest.

There he left her pregnant and forlorn;
Such sin is why this punishment condemns him,
And also for Medea the vengeance is done.

Those who are with him also deceived in the same way;
And this is sufficient to fill the first valley,
And those are the ones it holds in its jaws."

We came to where the narrow path
Crosses the second dike, and forms
Yet another arch.

Then we heard people, who are moaning
In the next circle, snorting with their noses,
And beating themselves with their hands.

The edges were incrusted with a mold
Made from the hot stench from below, which sticks
there,
And wages war with your eyes and nostrils.

The bottom is so deep, there is no place
That you can see, without ascending
The arch's back, and looking down.

There we came, and down in the moat
I saw people smothered in a filth
That seemed to flow out of human privates;

And while I was looking at those below,
I saw one with his head so foul with feces,
It was not clear if he was a clergyman or a layman.

He screamed to me: "Why are you so eager
To look at me more than the other foul ones?"

And I said to him: "Because, if I remember,

I have already seen you with dry hair,
And you are Alessio Interminei of Lucca;
That is why I see you more than I see the others."

And then he wiped his hand across his slimy head:
"Those types of flatteries have put me down here,
Especially when they came from my own tongue."

Then my Guide said to me:
"See that you look further ahead,
So that you will recognize another

Of that unclean and disheveled drab,
The one there that scratches herself with filthy nails,
And crouches and then stands again.

It is Thais the harlot, who replied
To her lover, when he asked, 'Am I worthy of your thanks?'
And she replied 'Again and again;'

And let that satisfy you for now."

INFERNO: CANTO XIX

O Simon Magus and your forlorn disciples,
The things of God, which should have been
Left on a path of holiness,

You prostitute them for silver and for gold,
And so the trumpet sounds for you,
Because now you live in this third circle.

We had already reached the edge of a tomb and
Ascended to that portion of the bridge
Which hangs over the middle of the moat.

Wisdom supreme, how great are your powers
In heaven, in earth, and in this evil hell,
And how appropriately justice distributes your power!

I saw on the sides and on the bottom
Of the stone, all of the perforations were filled,
They were all the same size, and everyone was round.

To me, they seemed neither lesser nor greater
Than those that are fashioned in my beautiful Saint John
For the place where the baptizers stand,

And one of which, not many years ago,
I broke for someone was drowning in it;
Let this be a sign for all men to be honest.

Out of the mouth of each of these, protruded
The feet of a transgressor, and the legs
Up to the calf. The rest remained hidden within.

In all of them both soles were on fire;
Which caused the ankles to quiver so violently,
They would have snapped any ropes or chains.

Even as a flame which is burning oily things
Will move along the outer surface only,

So the feet burned from heel to toe.

"Master, who is that one who is writhing
More than his other comrades"
I said, "And who has a redder flame burning?"

And he said to me: "If you want me to take you
Down there along that lowest bank, you will learn
From him what his sins were and who he is."

And I said: "Whatever pleases you, also pleases me;
You are my Lord, and know that I will not depart from
Your desire, for you know best even what is not spoken."

Then we arrived at the fourth circle;
We turned, and on the left side descended
Down to the bottom, which was narrow and full of holes.

And the good Master kept me at his side
Until he brought me to the hole which held
The one lamented so loud and shook his feet.

"Who are you, that is standing upside down,
O miserable soul, who is planted in the ground like a
Stake," I began, "If you can, speak to me."

I stood as a friar who is hearing the confession
Of an assassin, who, when he is fixed to die,
Calls him over, so that his death will be delayed.

And he cried out: "Have you already arrived here,
Do you stand there already, Boniface?
The record lied to me by many years.

Are you satiated with your wealth so soon,
For which you did not fear to take from the church,
By fraud, in order to work your woe?"

I became, as people who stand,
Not comprehending the answer they received,
As if being mocked, and not knowing not how to reply.

Then Virgil said: "Answer him. Say, 'I am not him, I am not who You think I am.'" And I replied as he instructed me.
This made the spirit kick with both his feet, then, sighing,

With a voice of lamentation he said to me: "Then what do you want Of me? If you want to know who I am, so much that you have crossed The bank, know that I once wore the papal crown;

And truly I was the son of the bear,
So eager to pocket the riches of that wealth
Above, and here, I find myself pocketed.

Beneath my head the others were dragged down
Who have preceded me in simony,
Flattened along the fissure of the rock.

Below there I will also fall, whenever
The one will come who I believed you were,
When I first asked the question.

But my feet have already been toasted,
And I have been in here upside down,
Longer than he will be planted with his reddened feet;

For after him shall come the fouler one
From the west, a Pastor who is without law,
And he will cover both of us.

He will be the New Jason, of whom we read
In Maccabees; and as his king was pliable,
So France's king will soften to this one."

I do not know if I was too bold,
When I answered him in this way:
"I pray that you tell me now how great a treasure

Our Lord demanded of Saint Peter first,

Before he put the keys into his keeping?
Truly he asked nothing more than to 'Follow me.'

Neither Peter nor the rest asked Matthew for
Silver or gold, when he was chosen
To fill the place the evil soul had lost.

Therefore stay here, for you are justly punished,
And keep safe guard over your ill-gotten money,
Which caused you to be valiant against Charles.

And if I did not have the
Reverence for the keys that you once held
In keeping in your happy life,

I would utter more grievous words still;
Because your avarice afflicts the world,
Trampling the good and lifting the depraved.

The Evangelist had you Pastors in mind,
When he spoke of she who sits upon many waters
And was seen to fornicate with many kings;

The same who was born with the seven heads,
And received power and strength from the ten horns,
So long as virtue was pleasing to her spouse.

You have made yourselves a god of gold and silver;
And are the same as someone who worships an idol,
Except that he worships one, and you worship a
hundred.

Ah, Constantine! What evil did you bring forth,
Not from your conversion, but from that marriage dowry
Which the first wealthy Father took from you!"

And while I spoke to him this way,
Either my anger or his own conscience stung him,
And he struggled violently with both his feet.

I think that it pleased my Leader, for

With a contented smile, he listened to every
True word that I expressed.

Therefore with both his arms he took me up,
And when he had me pressed against his chest,
Returned up the path the same way where we descended.

And he did not grow tired of having me clasped to him;
But took me to the summit of the arch
Which was the passage from the fourth circle to the fifth.

There he set me down,
Tenderly on the bridge uneven and steep,
That would have been a hard passage, even for goats:

There another valley was unveiled to me.

INFERNO: CANTO XX

I must try to find words
In order to best describe the new torments I see
As I have done with all the others, from the beginning.

By now, I have become accustomed
To looking down into the circles. The floor of this one
Was bathed with tears of agony;

And the people I saw in the circular valley,
Were silent and weeping, coming at a pace
Which other processions in this world assume.

As I looked closer at them,
Each one seemed to be distorted
From the chin to the beginning of the chest;

For towards the back their faces were turned,
And so backward they were forced to advance,
Because the ability to look forward was taken from them.

Maybe by violence caused by palsy
Someone could be turned around this way;
But I never saw it, nor believe it can be done.

If God allows you, Reader, to gather fruit
From this reading, think for yourself
How I could ever keep my eyes from crying,

When I saw people like myself distorted this way,
The weeping from their eyes flowed along the fissure
Of their back and bathed their backsides.

Truly I wept, leaning upon a peak
Of the hard crag, so that my Escort said
To me: "Are you, too, like the other fools?

Here pity lives when it should be dead;
Who is more evil than he

Who feels compassion at the ultimate doom?

Lift up your head, and see who
Opened the earth before the Thebans' eyes;
When they all cried: 'Where are your rushing to,

Amphiaraus? Why do you leave the war?'
And he continued to run and to fall
As far as Minos, who catches everyone.

See, he has turned his back into his chest!
Because he wished to see so far ahead of him
That he now looks behind, and goes his way backward:

And there is Tiresias, who changed his gender,
From a male to a female,
And all of his parts were transformed;

And afterwards, he was forced to strike again
The two entangled snakes with his rod,
Before he could regain his manly parts.

There is Aruns, who backs against the other's belly,
Who in the hills of Luni, where the Carrarese work
And lived beneath,

In a cavern in the white marble
Had his house; so that he could behold the stars
And sea, and the view would not be cut off from him.

And she there, who is covering up her breasts,
Which you cannot see, with her loosened tresses,
That, turned backwards, cover her front parts,

Is Manto, who traveled through many lands,
Afterwards stopping where I was born;
Now I will tell you a little about her.

After her father had departed from life,
And the city of Bacchus had become enslaved,
For a long time, she wandered through the world.

Above beautiful Italy lies a lake
At the Alp's foot that shuts in Germany
Over Tyrol, and is called Benaco.

And it is filled by a thousand springs, I think, maybe more,
Between Garda and Val Camonica,
With water that grows stagnant in that lake.

Midway is a place where the Trentine Pastor,
Of Brescia, and the Veronese
Might give his blessing, if he passed that way.

Peschiera, the fortress fair and strong, sits
To protect from the Brescians and the Bergamasks,
Where the bank is at its lowest.

There is where the excess water flows
When Benaco cannot hold any more,
And so a river flows down through the green pastures.

As soon as the water begins to run,
It is no longer called Benaco, but Mincio,
As far as Governo, where it flows into the Po.

Before too long, it finds a plain
In which it spreads itself, and makes it marshy,
And often in summer it brings sickness.

Passing that way the pitiless virgin land
In the middle of the plain described,
Lays untilled and naked of inhabitants;

There to escape all human encounters,
She with her servants stayed, to practice her arts
And to live. There, she left her empty body.

After that, the men, who were scattered around,
Gathered in that place, which was made strong
By the lagoon it had on every side;

They built their city over those dead bones,
And, they called it Mantua, after she who first
Selected the place, without any other sign.

Its people were more crowded once they were inside,
Before the stupidity of Casalodi
Who was deceived by Pinamonte.

Therefore I caution you, if ever you hear
That my city was born otherwise,
Do not let the lies conceal the truth."

And I said: "Master, your words are certain to me,
And have my faith, so that to me,
The words of others would be worthless.

But tell me of the people who are passing us now,
If you see anyone who is note-worthy,
For my mind reverts back to that."

Then he said to me: "He who thrusts his beard
Upon his massive shoulders was a soothsayer,
At the time when there were no more males in Greece,

So that there were even few remaining in the cradle,
He with Calchas gave the command,
In Aulis, to launch the fleet.

His name was Eryphylus, and I told his story in
My lofty Tragedy in one place or other;
But you already know that, you have read the entire
piece.

The next, who is so slender in the legs,
Was Michael Scott, who, through a variety
Of magical illusions, knew the game.

There is Guido Bonatti, and Asdente,
Who now wishes he had stuck to his leather and his
thread,

But it is too late for him to repent.

See the wretched ones, who left the needle,
The spool and the rock, and made themselves fortune-
tellers;
They brought their magic spells with herbs and images.

But come now, for Cain and the thorns, confine
Both of the hemispheres, and under Seville
Touches the ocean waves,

Last night the moon was already full;
You should remember well that it helped you
From time to time when you were within the deep
forest."

Thus he spoke to me, and we walked on.

INFERNO: CANTO XXI

We walked from one bridge to the next bridge,
Speaking of many things that I will not include here.
When we came to the summit of the bridge,

We stopped to see another group
Of Malebolge and heard other vain laments;
And I noticed that it was suddenly very dark.

As in the Arsenal of the Venetians
When they boil pitch in the winter
To smear on their leaky vessels to repair them,

Because they are too badly damaged to sail;
And instead of making a new ship, they patch
The ribs of older ones that have already made many voyages;

One hammers at the prow, one at the stern,
This one makes oars, and that one makes ropes,
Another mends the mainsail and another, the mizzen;

Not by fire, but by divine intervention,
The dense pitch below us was boiling
And covered all sides of the bank.

I saw it, but I could not see what was in it
Except for the bubbles that the boiling raised,
Which swelled up and then burst and subsided.

While I gazed fixedly at the activity below,
My Leader, crying out: "Look out, Look out!"
And pulled me back to him.

Then I turned around, as one who is impatient
To see what it was that concerned him,
And what would cause a man to become suddenly afraid,

And who, while still looking back, continues to run;

And I saw behind us a black devil,
Running along the ridge, and coming towards us quickly.

He looked ferocious in both his appearance and his movements!
And he seemed as though he was going to attack,
With open wings and swift feet!

His shoulders, were high and sharply pointed,
And he held a sinner closely to his body,
Clutching him tightly with his claws.

From our bridge he shouted: "O Malebranche,
Look, here is one of the elders of Saint Zita;
Keep him down in the pitch, and I will go get more

From that place, which has so many of them.
They are all a bunch of cheaters, except Bonturo;
'No' is changed into 'Yes' for the right amount of money."

He hurled him down over the hard ledge and
Turned round. Never was a hound, when turned loose,
In so much of a hurry to pursue a thief.

The other sank into the pitch, and rose again face downward;
But the demons, under cover of the bridge,
Cried: "This is not the place for those actions!

The swimming is very different here than in the Serchio;
Unless you want to feel the sharp ends of our pitch forks,
You will not lift yourself out of the pitch."

They stabbed him with over a hundred forks; and shouted:
"You will learn that it is best to stay covered in pitch,
You will have to do your cheating under the surface."

They stabbed him again as cooks make their apprentices
Push the meat down into the middle of the pot
With their forks so that it does not float.

The good Master said to me:
"They must not know that you are here, crouch down
Behind a pillar, so that it will keep you hidden;

And no matter what they may do to me
Do not be afraid, because I know these creatures.
I was in a scuffle with them before."

Then he walked to the end of the bridge,
And stepped on to the bank of the sixth circle,
He stood straight and still, but showed his courage.

With the same fury, and the same uproar,
As dogs leap out upon a weak beggar,
Making him stop and stay where he stands,

The devils flew out from beneath the little bridge,
And turned against him with their pitch forks;
But he cried out: "Stop it. All of you!

Before you lay those hooks of yours on me,
One of you should listen well to what I have to say,
And then decide if you think it is wise to attack."

They all cried out: "Let Malacoda go speak with him;"
Then Malacoda stepped forward, and the rest stayed back,
And he approached my master saying:

"And how will your words help you?"
"Do you think, Malacoda, that I could have
Advanced so far into this place," My Master said,

"Safe and unharmed against all opposition, without the aid And assistance of God? Let me pass, for Heaven has willed
That I escort another person along this savage road."

Then Malacoda's arrogance faded away,
And he dropped his pitchfork at his feet,

He turned to the others and said:

"Nobody touch him." And my Guide called to me:
"You, who are crouched down behind the pillars
Of the bridge, you can safely come to me now."

I stood up quickly and ran to him;
And all the devils lunged forward at the same time,
So that I was afraid they would not keep their word.

I remember seeing the fear in the eyes of soldiers
Though passing under a flag of truce from Caprona,
As they moved along past so many of the enemy soldiers.

I pressed myself very close
To my Leader's side, but did not take my eyes
From their faces which looked at me very sternly.

They lowered their pitchforks at me, and said
"Do you think I should take a stab at him?"
Then another one said, "On the rump?"

And another one answered: "Yes; See if you can
Poke him there."But the same demon who had spoken
With my Master turned very quickly, and said:

"Shut your mouth, Scarmiglione; Be quiet." Then said
to Us: "You cannot go any further on this bridge,
Because It Is lying shattered at the bottom of the sixth
circle.

But if you insist on going forward,
Make your way along this rock;
Near here is another bridge on the path.

In five hours, it will be exactly
One thousand two hundred and sixty-six
Years and one day, that this bridge was broken.

I will send some of my men to escort you
To make sure that you are not bothered along your way;

Go with them. They will not harm you.

Step forward, Alichino and Calcabrina,"
He began to cry out, "And you, Cagnazzo;
And Barbariccia, you will lead them.

Come forward, Libicocco and Draghignazzo,
And Ciriatto with the jagged teeth and Graffiacane,
And Farfarello and Rubicante the furious;

Take them around this boiling pitch;
And keep them safe as far as the next bridge
Which is still unbroken over the next circle."

"Master, I don't trust them. Please, just the two of us
Should go." I said, "We don't need an escort,
If you know the way, that is good enough for me.

If you are as observant as you always have been,
You can see that they gnash their teeth,
And look at us with threats in their eyes."

And he said to me: "You need not be afraid of them;
Let them gnash their teeth, if it makes them happy,
Because they do it for those boiling wretches, not us."

Along the left side of the dike they wheeled around;
But before we left, one of them stuck his tongue out
At their leader;

And the leader replied with a loud fart.

INFERNO: CANTO XXII

I have seen horsemen moving camp,
Begin the attack, and review their troops,
And sometimes, I have even seen them in retreat;

I have seen scouts exploring the land,
Raiding parties sacking villages, holding tournaments,
And jousting between men, and each carries its own signal.

Sometimes with trumpets and sometimes with bells,
With kettle-drums, and fires from the castles,
And many common and outlandish things,

But I have never seen a group set out, nor horsemen move,
Nor infantry march, nor ship set sail,
No matter how uncouth, with such a blast as we had received.

We went on our way with the ten demons;
What a savage company it was! But, when in the church
You are with saints, and in the tavern, with the gluttons!

I was constantly watching the boiling pitch,
To better understand what was happening in this circle,
And to the people who were punished there.

Even as dolphins, when they make a sign
To mariners by arching their back,
That they should be careful when sailing their vessel,

Sometimes here, to alleviate his pain,
One of the sinners would arch his back,
But would instantly pull it back down.

As frogs sit at the edge of the water in a ditch
Completely submerged, with only their muzzles out,
So that they can hide their feet and bodies,

Everywhere, here, the sinners sat;
But as soon as Barbariccia came near them,
They would dive underneath the boiling pitch.

I saw, and my heart still shudders at the thought,
One sinner waiting, even sometimes as
One frog remains, and another dives down;

And Graffiacan, standing in front of him,
Grabbed him by his pitch smeared hair,
And pulled him up, so that he looked like an otter.

I knew the names of all of our troop,
As I had memorized them when they were chosen,
And when they spoke to each other, I listened as well.

"Hey Rubicante, see that you grab him with
Your claws, so that you can rip his skin off."
Our troop cried out to him. And I said:
"Master, if at all possible, can you find out
Who that unlucky sinner is,
That is held in his adversaries' hands."

My Leader stepped up close to him,
And asked him who he was; and he replied:
"I was born in the kingdom of Navarre;

My mother placed me in the service of a lord,
Because my father was a dishonest knave,
Who destroyed all that he owned before he killed
himself.

Then I was a servant for good King Thibault;
And he taught me how to steal,
Which now has me burning in this boiling pitch."

And Ciriatto, who had a tusk projecting from each side
Of his mouth, like a boar,
Gored the man and began to rip off his skin.

This poor mouse had fallen among malicious cats;
But Barbariccia clasped Ciriatto by his arms,
And said: "Stand aside, while I stab him."

He turned to face my master; "Ask him again,"
He said, "If you want to know any more from him,
Before one of us destroys him."

My Guide said: "Tell us of the other sinners;
Do you know of any Italians stuck there,
Under the pitch?" And he said:

"I was just with someone who was from that area;
I wish I were still covered up with him,
For then I would not be clawed or gored!"

And Libicocco said: "We have heard enough;"
And with his pitch fork, he stabbed him in the arm,
Then twisting hard, he tore off a piece of flesh.

Draghignazzo wanted a piece of him as well,
He tried to grab a leg; when their leader
Turned around and gave him an evil look.

The others started to back away now.
The sinner was still looking at his wound,
When my Master asked him:

"Who was the person you spoke of? The one you left
When you were dragged ashore?"
And he replied: "It was the Friar Gomita,

He was from Gallura, the place filled with fraud,
When the enemies of his lord were captured,
They were very pleased with their treatment;

He would take money from them and send them on their way,
As he tells it; But he was not a petty thief
For all of his stealing was from noblemen.

He now sits with Don Michael Zanche
Of Logodoro; and they gossip of Sardinia
But their tongues never get tired.

O me! See that one, how he grinds his teeth;
I would say more, but I am afraid
That he is getting ready to gore me again."

And then their leader, turned to Farfarello,
Who rolled his eyes as if ready to strike,
And said: "You stay right there, you filthy hawk."

"If you want to either see or hear more,"
The terror-stricken sinner continued,
"Tuscans or Lombards, I can make them come.

But have the Malebranche back away a little,
So that the new comers will not fear being ripped apart,
I will sit right here in this spot,

And I will call. Seven of them will come,
When I whistle, as it is our custom
To do when it is safe to come out of the pit."

Cagnazzo lifted his muzzle listened when he heard this.
Shaking his head, he said: "Did you all hear the trick that he Is playing on us? He is lying so that we will set him free!"

And the sinner replied:
"I agree with you that I have many tricks,
But that would just bring more trouble to my friends."

Alichino could not resist the challenge, and, not caring what the others thought, cried out: "If you think that you can escape, then try. I will not come running for you,

But I will fly past you and beat you to the pitch;
We will leave this area, and stand behind the hill.
And then we will see just how fast you are."

To you, dear reader, this was suddenly a new game!
Each of them turned away from their prisoner;
And the first to turn was the one who was most reluctant.

The Navarrese chose his time well;
He planted his feet on the ground, and in a moment
Leaped, and rushed away from them.

Suddenly each one of them swung around, stung with shame,
But the one that stung the most he who caused
Them to lose. He ran and cried out; "I've got you now."

But it was no use, for his wings were not
As fast as the others fear; the sinner dove into the pitch,
And the flyer had to pull up quickly;

Just like a duck which will suddenly
Dive under, when the falcon is approaching,
Causing the falcon to pull back, cross and weary.

Infuriated at the mockery, Calcabrina
Flying close behind him, hoped that the sinner would escape
So that you would have a reason to quarrel with Alchino.

And when the sinner disappeared,
He turned his talons on his companion,
And grappled with him above the boiling moat.

But his opponent was a hawk as well and had his own
Set of claws; With both fighting and neither flying,
They fell in the middle of the boiling pond.

The heat was quick to separate them;
But nevertheless neither of them could fly,
Because their wings were bogged down in pitch.

As upset as the others, Barbariccia
Made four of them fly quickly to the other side
With their pitch forks.

The ones on this side also lowered their forks;
They all stretched their hooks towards the ones caught,
In the pitch, who were already baking in the crust,

And that is how we left them.

INFERNO: CANTO XXIII

We walked onward, silent, alone, and without company,
One in front, the other behind,
As Minor Friars going along their way.

When I was thinking about the quarrel we had just seen,
It reminded me of Aesop's fable
About the frog and mouse;

For what happened then and what happened now
Could not have been more alike if you compare
The Beginning and The End of the events.

And as one thought springs from another,
And after that, yet a different thought,
The fear inside of me began to double. I was thinking:

"These demons were laughed at and scorned because of
us. They were not only tricked, but injured as well
And they will be very annoyed with us.

If angry thoughts become vengeful actions,
They will come after us more merciless
Than a dog chasing a rabbit."

I felt my hair stand on end
With terror, and stood looking backward,
When said I: "Master, I think that we should hide

From the Malebranche,
I am afraid that they are right behind us;
I can almost feel them there." And he said:

"Even if I were a mirror,
I could not reflect your outer terror
Any faster than I can already feel your inner fear.

Just now, your thoughts came to me,
And they were very similar to my own,

So that both of us were in agreement before you spoke.

If we find a place ahead where the right bank slopes
So that we can descend into the circle,
We will be escape from the chase you think is coming."

He had barely finished speaking,
When I saw them coming with outstretched wings,
Not very far away, and they were heading towards us.

My Leader seized me at once,
Like a mother, awakened by a noise,
And sees flames close behind her,

Who takes her son, and flies, and does not stop,
Caring more for him than for herself,
Not even stopping to grab her own clothing;

And from the top of the bank, he dragged me,
Sliding along the rocky path, holding me to his chest,
Down the side of the circle wall.

Water never ran so swiftly through a sluice
To turn the wheel of any mill,
When it approaches the paddles,

As my Master slid down along that bank,
Riding on his back, bearing me on his chest,
As he would his own son, and not as a companion.

We had barely reached the bed of the ravine below
When the flying devils arrived on the hill
Right above us; but he was not afraid;

For the Divine Powers, which had ruled that they
Be the ministers of the fifth circle,
Left them powerless to pursue us in the sixth.

Here in our new circle, we found people who were painted,
Who walked along very slowly,

Weeping and tired as though vanquished.

They had on robes with the hoods pulled low
Over their eyes, and fashioned similar
To those worn by the monks of Cologne.

Outside, they were gilded so it dazzled in the faint light;
But inside, they are filled with lead and so heavy
That Frederick would put them on straw to keep it in place.

Oh what a cloak of everlasting fatigue!
Again we turned, as before, to the left
And walked along with them, watching this sad group;

But because of the weight that made them so weary,
They moved very slowly, so that we were always in a new
Group every time we took a step.

I said to my Leader:
"If you find someone who I might know by name or deed,
Please point them out to me."

And one, who understood what I had asked,
Cried out from behind us: "Stay where you are,
You who are running though this heavy air!

Perhaps you will get what you want from me."
My Leader turned to me, and said:
"Wait, and we will walk with him at his pace."

I stopped, and saw two of them hurrying to join us,
The strain showing in their faces; But they were slowed down
By the burden they carried and the narrow path.

When they caught up, they looked at me for a long time
Without uttering a word.
Then they looked at each other and one said:

"The way that his throat is moving, he appears to be alive;
And if they are dead, what gives them the privilege
To be here without having to wear this heavy robe?"

Then he said to me: "Tuscan, who has come to the college
Of miserable hypocrites,
Tell us who you are." And I said to them:

"I was born, and grew up
In the great town on the Arno river,
And I am here with the body that I have always had.

But who are you, with your tears trickling down
Along your cheeks from such grief?
And what pain do you carry that sparkles so much?"

And one replied to me: "These orange cloaks
Are made of lead so heavy, that the weight of them
Causes us, who carry them, to creak when we walk.

We were Jovial Friars, and Bolognese;
I am Catalano, and he is Loderingo,
We were taken together by your city,

Though they usually take only one man alone,
To maintain peace; and what we did
Can still be seen around Gardingo."

"Oh Friars," I began, "Your wickedness. . ."
But then I stopped; for I was distracted by
A man on the ground crucified with three stakes.

When he saw me, he began writhing all over,
Breathing through his beard with heavy gasps;
Friar Catalano noticed my gaze and said to me:

"This transfixed one, that you see there,
Advised the Pharisees that it was better
To torture one man, Jesus, than to lose a nation.

Now he himself is naked and on the cross,
As you see; and he feels the weight
Of whoever walks past him;

His father-in-law is punished in similar fashion
Within this circle, as are the others of the council,
Which were the seed of evil for the Jews."

And I saw Virgil marvel
At the man who was extended on the cross
Punished so violently in eternal banishment.

Then he said to the Friar:
"If you do not mind, can you tell us
If any pass along here slopes down to the right?

That way, we can leave here,
Without having the black angels
Come and pull us from this cavern."

He answered: "Closer than you think,
There is a rock, that leads out of this great circle,
And crosses all of the cruel valleys,

Except this one, over which it is broken;
You will be able to climb up the ruins,
That rise from the bottom of this pit."

The Leader stood awhile with his head bowed down;
Then said: " He lied to us. The one who punishes the
Sinners up there." And the Friar said:

"I have heard many of the Devil's vices
When I was at Bologna, and among them is
That he is a liar and the father of lies."

My Leader moved on, taking great strides.
He looked somewhat disturbed with anger;
I also turned and left the heavy-laden Friars

Trying to keep up and follow in his footprints.

INFERNO: CANTO XXIV

In the early part of the year
When the sun rises in Aquarius,
And the nights are almost as long as the days,

When the morning frost on the ground
Looks like newly fallen snow,
But only lasts for a little while,

The Sheppard, who has no food for his animals,
Rises, and looks, and sees the fields
Gleaming white, raises his fists in anger,

Returns indoors, and paces back and forth,
Like a poor wretch, who does not know what to do;
But when he returns, his hope revives again.

Seeing that the world has changed in the blink of an eye
He takes his shepherd's crook,
And drives the young lambs to pasture.

This sense of alarm filled me as well,
When I saw that my Master was so disturbed,
But the treatment came almost as fast as the ailment.

Because, as we came up to the ruined bridge,
The Leader turned to me with that sweet look
Which I first saw at the mountain's foot.

His took a long look, assessed the ruins,
And after thinking for a moment,
His arms opened and he picked me up.

And as someone who thinks first and then acts,
Always prepared for what he is going to do next,
So he carried me upward towards the summit of a huge rock.

He looked around at the other rocks, saying:

"We will climb to that next one,
But first, make sure it will hold you."

This was no way to travel for someone wearing a cloak;
Even though he was light, and I had his help,
We were barely able to climb from rock to rock.

And had it not been, that this bank was
Shorter than the one we came down,
I don't know about him, but I would have failed.

But because Malebolge slope down,
Pointing always to the well in the center,
The structure of each valley is such that

As the outer bank rises, the inner bank sinks.
After great effort, we finally reached
The top of the broken pathway of stone.

The breath had completely vanished from my lungs, so that,
When I got to the top of the broken rock, I could go no more.
I sat down on the ground and did not move.

"Now is not the time for rest,"
My Master said; "No one ever gained fame,
By staying under a quilt,

And without fame, a man must try to leave his mark
In whatever vestige of himself he can put on earth, but
That is like leaving smoke in the air, or foam on the water.

So, come on, get up, overcome your pain
With the spirit that overcomes every battle,
So long as the body still supports it.

You will be climbing an even longer stairway later;
And we still have more sinners to see;
You know what I am talking about. Come on, let's go."

Then I got up, seeing that I could now catch my breath
Better that I thought I would be able to,
And said: "Let's go.   I am ready now, and much
stronger."

Upward we climbed along the edge,
Which was jagged, and narrow, and difficult,
And far more precipitous than the part we just climbed.

I kept talking, not wanting to appear exhausted;
When I heard a voice coming from the next moat.
A voice that had trouble speaking the words.

I do not know what it said, though I was at the top
Of the arch that passes there;
But whoever was speaking, seemed angry.

I was bent down, but my eyes
Could not see the bottom, because it was so dark;
I said: "Master, let's go to the next round,

And we will descend that wall;
For I am hearing something and do not understand it,
And when I look down, I can see nothing."

"I can give you no answer," He said,
"Except by doing what you ask; because such a request
Is best followed by action rather than answer."

We walked down to the foot of the bridge,
Where it connects with the eighth bank,
And before me was the next circle;

There I saw a terrible throng
Of serpents, and they were so monstrous,
That just remembering them still chills my blood

Libya can no longer boast of her mass expanse of sand;
For though she carries Chelydri, Jaculi, and Phareae
And Cenchres with Amphisbaena,

She never had plagues so numerous nor so horrible,
Even combined with those that appeared in all of Ethiopia,
And around the Red Sea, as what I saw below.

Among this cruel and dismal throng
People were running naked and afraid.
Without the hope of refuge or cover.

They had their hands bound behind them with serpents;
These serpents girdled their chest and loins
And coiled around their bodies from head to tail.

Suddenly, a sinner ran past us on the bank and immediately
A serpent shot forth and grabbed him with his fangs,
Right where the neck is connected to the shoulders.

Never was a word put to paper as fast this duo
Burst into flames and burned;
The ashes fell to the ground in a crumpled heap.

And when the group was destroyed, and laying on the ground,
The ashes drew together, and by themselves
Instantly returned to their prior form.

Even as the great sages have said that
The phoenix dies, and then is born again from its ashes,
When it approaches its five-hundredth year;

During its life, it does not feed on herb or grain,
But only on tears of incense and spice,
And finally wrapping itself in nard and myrrh.

As he who falls, but knows not how,
By the force of demons who drag them down to earth,
Or by other obstructions that will bind man,

When he gets up and looks around, he is completely

Bewildered by the mighty anguish which he has suffered,
Sometimes moaning and rubbing his pains;

This is how the sinner was after he had risen.
Oh how severe is the justice of God,
That blows like these pour down in vengeance!

The Guide asked him who he was;
And he replied: "I was from Tuscany
A short time before falling into this cruel gorge.

Just like the mule that I was; I loved the life of a beast,
And not of a human; I am Vanni Fucci, the Savage Beast,
And Pistoia was a den worthy of my kind."

And I said to the Guide: "Tell him not to move,
And ask what crime has put him down here,
For I once knew him as a man of wrath and of blood."

And the sinner did not try to hide that he had heard me,
But turned and looked me directly in the face,
And his face reddened with his melancholy shame.

Then he said: "It pains me more that you have caught me
Amid this misery where you now see me,
Than when I was taken from the other life.

What you have said, I cannot deny;
I was put here, so far down, because I robbed
The church of its treasures,

And the crime was falsely laid upon another;
But do not rejoice in seeing me here,
If you ever get out of these dark places,

Open your ears and listen to what I have to say:
Pistoia will first throw out the members of the Black
party;
Then Florence will rebuild both her men and laws;

Mars will draw a mist up from Val di Magra,

Which will be enveloped all around with horrible clouds,
And with a savage and bitter storm.

Over Piceno's fields there be a great battle;
When lightning will suddenly rip through the mist,
So that each member of the White party will be
wounded.

Know that I have told you this in order to hurt you."

INFERNO: CANTO XXV

When he was done speaking, the thief
Shook his fists at the heavens and cried:
"Take that, God, these words are for you!"

After that, the serpents were my friends;
For one entwined itself around his neck
As if to say: "You have said enough;"

And another went around his arms, and pinned him,
Clinching themselves together in front,
So that he could no longer move.

Pistoia, oh, Pistoia! Why not just
Burn yourself to ashes and die,
Since your children are worse than you were?

Through all of the horrid circles of this Hell,
I had never seen a Spirit so proud to be against God,
Not even the one who fell from the walls at Thebes!

He fled away, and did not speak again;
And I saw a Centaur full of rage
Come crying out: "Where is he? Where is the scoffer?"

I do not think Maremma has as many
Serpents as he had all along his back,
Right up to where his human form begins.

On his shoulders, just behind the nape,
With wings wide open, was a dragon,
And he blew fire at anything that he saw.

My Master said: "That one is Cacus, who, many times,
Has created a lake of blood
Beneath the rock on Mount Aventine

He does not go on the same road with his brothers,
Because of the cunning way that he stole

The great herd of cattle, which was near his land;

His tortuous actions ended beneath
The mace of Hercules, who probably
Gave him a hundred blows, though he felt only ten."

While he was speaking, Cacas had moved on,
And three spirits appeared underneath us,
That neither I, nor my leader, were aware of,

Until they shouted: "Who are you two?"
At which point our talking ended,
And we began watching them.

I did not know them; but soon,
As happens sometimes,
One was compelled to call the other by name,

Exclaiming: "Where is Cianfa?"
So that my Leader would notice,
I pressed my finger against my lips to remain silent.

If you are, dear Reader, slow to believe
What I am telling you, I completely understand,
Because even though I saw it, I can hardly believe it.

As I was watching them,
A lizard, with six feet, shot up
In front of one, and fastened on to him.

The middle feet latched on to his stomach
And the front ones grabbed his arms;
It thrust its teeth through one cheek and then the other;

The back feet were stretched around his thighs,
Then slid its tail between his legs,
And up along his back.

Ivy was never fastened
Onto a tree so tightly, as this horrible reptile
Entwined its own limbs upon the other's.

They were pressed close together, as if made of heated wax
So that even their color was mixed together;
And neither one seemed to be what he was before;

Just as flame moving along paper
Proceeds up, pushing a brown color,
Which is not yet black, but the white has died.

The other two looked on, and each of them cried out:
"O my, Agnello, how you have changed!
You are no longer two, but not yet one."

Already the two heads had become one,
And there appeared to be two figures mingled
Into one face, their individual features lost.

The four arms were mingled into two arms,
The thighs and legs, the belly and the chest
Each merging into parts never before seen.

Every original feature was merged or cancelled;
Two creatures merged, but neither looked like the original,
And then it turned and slowly walked away.

Like a lizard, under the massive heat
Of a Summer's day, runs from hedge to hedge,
Shoots across a road like a bolt of lightning;

Suddenly there appeared, aiming at the bellies
Of the other two, a small fiery lizard,
Full of rage and black as pepper.

It leaped up, without notice,
And bit into the stomach of one of the ghosts;
Then fell to the ground again.

The one who had been bitten stood still, saying nothing;
He stood perfectly still and then yawned,

As if sleep or fever had suddenly overcome him.

He looked at the lizard, and the lizard looked at him;
Violent smoke came from both of them, one through the stomach,
The other through the mouth, and the smoke commingled.

Lucan once tried to explain this, where he mentions
Wretched Sabellus and Nassidius,
But wait until you hear what I saw.

And also Ovid, telling of the change of Cadmus and Arethusa;
For he changed into a snake, her into a fountain,
As each underwent their conversion, I do not envy him;

Because two creatures never, facing each other,
Transformed, so that both of the beings
Would somehow change into the other.

This is what these two were doing,
The lizards tail split into two,
And the wounded man's feet grew together.

Then the legs and thighs became one,
So that soon, they were merged
Leaving no sign that they were ever separated.

The lizard began his transformation into a man.
His skin was becoming elastic
While the other one was growing scales.

I saw the arms of one draw in at the armpits,
And on the reptile, the feet were beginning to form,
Lengthening as much as the other's contracted.

Then, the lizard's hind feet came forward and merged,
To become the man's private parts,
And the man's part split in two and became legs.

The smoke barely concealed them,
Changing colors, and bringing out hair on one
And removing it from the other,

Finally, one rose up, and the other fell,
But they continued to look at each other,
And under their eyes, their faces changed.

He who was now standing, his face grew narrow,
And from the extra skin that he had,
Ears were formed;

And from the extra that was not used,
A nose began to grow on his face,
And his lips thickened.

The one who was laying down also was changing,
His ears drew back into his head,
Just like the horns of a snail;

And his tongue, which was used for speech before,
Was split down the center, while in the other one,
It merged into one. Then the smoke cleared.

The soul, which had been changed into a reptile,
Scampered along the valley in flight,
The other one began speaking in sputters.

Then he turned his head, and said to the other:
"Now it is time for Buoso to run,
Crawling as I have done, along this road."

This is how things shifted in the seventh circle,
And I apologize if I did not explain it well, it is because
It was new to me, and words fall short on such things.

And though my eyes might be somewhat bewildered,
And my mind dismayed,
They could not hide from me

That I plainly saw Puccio Sciancato;

The sole survivor of the three companions,
Which came to us in the beginning, and was not changed;

Was also the one that made Gaville weep.

INFERNO: CANTO XXVI

Rejoice, Florence, for you are truly great,
Your reach extends over land and sea,
And throughout Hell your name is known everywhere!

Among the thieves, I found five of your citizens,
Which brings me great shame,
And does not reflect well on your honor.

But if in the morning our dreams come true,
In the near future, you will feel
What Prato and the others crave for you.

If it happened right now, it would not be too soon;
It should have already happened, but it will happen,
Until it does, it grieves me more, the older I get.

We went our way, up along the stairs
The rocks had made, where us descended before,
Led by my Conductor and me following behind.

And we moved along the solitary path
Among the rocks and ridges of the circle,
Using both our feet and hands to move forward.

Then I felt sad, and the sorrow spread,
When I think about all that I have seen,
And I had to keep my thoughts in check, more than I wanted,

But I will not convey it unless virtue makes me;
So that if a good star, or something else,
Has brought me luck, then I will not refuse it.

As people who stay behind (as those who rest on the hill
After the sun, which lights the world
Has fallen beyond our sight,

While the firefly takes the place of the gnat)

See the glowing fires down along the valley,
Maybe down where he ploughs or makes his wine;

That is how many flames I saw
In the eighth circle, which I grew aware of
As soon as I was able to see over the edge.

And as the prophet who was devoured by bears
Saw Elijah's chariot leaving,
When his horses rose towards Heaven,

Though he could no longer see it
I was able to watch the flame ascend,
Like a little cloud climbing into the sky,

This is how the flames were moving at the bottom of the gorge.
Not one flame showed what it was consuming,
But I knew that each flame was consuming a sinner.

I stood on the bridge to see better,
And if I had not held on to a rock,
I would have fallen over the edge.

And the Leader, who watched me so intently,
Exclaimed: "The spirits are within the fires;
Each one burning in his flaming punishment."

"Master," I replied, "Though I already guessed that
This was happening, from what you have said
I am certain now, and would like to ask you

Who is in that fire, which is split
At the top, it seems to be burning like the fire
Where Eteocles was burned with his brother."

He answered me: "Within there are the tormented souls of
Ulysses and Diomed, and together
They feel the wrath of vengeance.

Within their flame, they lament
The ambush of the Trojan horse, which became the door
Where the Roman's were able to defeat Troy;

Together, they mourn the trick which still causes
Deidamia to weep for Achilles,
And they pay for the pain of taking the Palladium."

"If those within the sparks can speak,"
I said, "Master, please,
I pray to you a thousand times,

Let me wait until the horned flame comes closer;
As I would like to see it."
And he said to me:

"That is a worthy request
And therefore I will grant it;
But take heed that you do not say too much.

Let me speak, because I know what you wish to ask
And they might become upset
If they hear your accent, since they were Greeks."

The flame reached a point near us,
When my Leader seemed it appropriate,
And I finally heard him speak:

"You, who are two spirits within one fire,
While I was living,
If I deserved any praise

When I wrote the lofty verses,
Stop for a moment, and one of you tell me
Whether either of you died because of your own fault."

Then the greater of the two flames,
Began to murmur and wave itself about
Even as a flame does when it fights the wind.

Then the tip began moving to and fro

As if it were the tongue of a snake,
And it uttered in a voice saying: "When I

Had departed from Circe, who concealed me
For more than a year near Gaeta,
Before Aeneas gave it that name,

Not fondness for my son, nor reverence
For my old father, nor the due affection
Which should have made Penelope joyous,

Could overcome the desire within me,
I had to experience the world,
And the vice and virtue of mankind;

So I set sail on the open sea
With only one ship, and a small company of men
Who did not desert me.

I saw the shores as far as Spain,
As far as Morocco, and the isle of Sardinia,
And many other islands surrounded by the sea.

Me and my company were old and slow
When we arrived at that narrow passage
Where Hercules set his signals as landmarks,

So that no man should venture past them.
Behind me, on the right, I saw Seville,
And on the other I had already left Ceuta.

'Brothers, who have come through a hundred thousand
Perils,' I said, 'to reach the West,
On this inconceivable voyage

While we still retain our senses
Let us not deny ourselves the knowledge,
Of following the sun to the places no one has gone
before.

Consider where you came from;

You were not made to live like brutes,
But were made for the pursuit of virtue and of knowledge.'

So eager did I make my companions for the voyage,
With this brief speech,
That I could hardly have held them back.

And having turned our stern into the morning sun,
Our oars became our wings for our mad flight,
Always sailing to our left.

We could see the stars of the Southern pole
In the night, and our stars were so low
That they did not rise above the ocean floor.

Five times rekindled and as many times quenched
As we counted the fullness of the moon,
Since we had entered into the deep pass,

When there appeared a mountain,
In the distance, and it seemed to me higher
Then any I had ever seen before.

At first, we were joyful, but it soon turned to weeping;
Because a whirlwind arose out of the new land,
And smashed into the front part of the ship.

Three times it spun her in the waters,
And on the fourth turn, it raised the stern,
And submerged the bow,

Until the sea closed in above us."

INFERNO: CANTO XXVII

The flame was now straight and quiet,
It no longer spoke, and left us
With the permission of the gentle Poet;

Then another flame came up behind it,
Which made us look up at its top
Because of a strange sound coming from it.

Like the Sicilian bull
(That first bellowed
With the cries of the man who made it)

This flame bellowed with the sound of its sinner,
Granted, it was not made of brass,
But still it appeared transfixed with agony;

So, since it had no other way to express itself,
The sinner used the voice of the flames, and the sound
Was converted into his melancholy words.

When all of the words had gathered
Up at the top of the flame, it started to move
Similar to a tongue, and thus the sound was made,

We heard it say: "You, who can now hear the sound of
My voice, and who was speaking Lombard just now,
Saying to the other flame, 'Now you can go your way'

Even though I came a little late,
If you don't mind, will you stay and speak with me;
You see that it won't bother me, and I am burning.

If you have just arrived into this blind world
And have fallen down from that sweet Italian land,
Where I brought all of my transgressions,

Tell me if the Romagnols have peace or war,
Because I was from the mountains there between

Urbino and where the Tiber bursts through."

I was still bending downward to listen,
When my Conductor touched me on the side,
And said: "You should speak: this one is Italian."

I had already formed my reply
And so I began to speak:
"O soul, that is concealed below this flame,

Romagna is not and never has been
Free from war in the hearts of its tyrants;
But there was no open warfare when I left just now.

Ravenna stands as it has stood for many long years;
The Eagle of Polenta is brooding there,
Covering all of Cervia with her wings.

The city which was long known for its resistance,
And left the French in a bloody heap,
Now finds itself beneath the Green Claws once again;

Verrucchio's ancient Mastiff as well as the new one,
Who made such horrible leaders of Montagna,
Now sink their teeth into the people.

The cities of Lamone and Santerno
Are Governed by the Lion of the white lair,
Who changes sides more often than the seasons change;

And of the city which is bathed by the Savio,
Just as it lies between the plain and mountain,
It also lives between tyranny and a free state.

Now I ask you to tell us who you are;
Do not be more stubborn than the rest have been,
So that your name will be known in the world."

After the fire had roared a little more,
The sharp point moved this way and that
And then gave out a breath:

"If I thought that my answer was being made
To someone who would return to the world,
This flame would stop flickering and would stand still;

But since no one has ever returned from this depth,
If what I have heard in the past is true,
Then I will answer without fear,

I was a man of arms, then a friar,
Believing that by wearing the cord, I would repent;
And really, my belief would have been fulfilled

Except for the High Priest, who is probably burning down here,
Who put me back into my former sins;
I will tell you that happened.

While I was still alive on the Earth
The deeds I did where not those of a lion,
But rather, they were those of a fox.

I knew all of the actions and the covert ways,
And I practiced them so well,
That I was known far and wide to the ends of earth.

As I got older, and finally reached the age
When you should lower your sails
And coil away the ropes,

Those things that had pleased me then, now displeased me;
I was penitent and confessed my sins,
And became a friar! and it would have saved me;

But then, the Leader of the modern Pharisees
Decided to wage war on the Lateran,
Instead of the Saracens or the Jews,
For each one of his enemies was Christian,
Not the ones who fought for the church,
Nor those who were merchants in the Sultan's land,

He had no regard for his high office,
Nor his sacred vows, nor in the rope of a Friar
Which we wore to show our devotion;

But even as Constantine had looked for Sylvester
To cure his leprosy, within Soracte,
So this one sought me out as his doctor

To cure him of the fever of his pride.
He asked me for advice, and I was silent,
Because his words sounded like drunken speech.

And then he said: 'Don't be afraid; After you are done,
I will absolve you of your sins; now tell me
How to raze Palestrina to the ground.

I have the power to lock and to unlock Heaven,
As you know; I have both keys,
The ones which my predecessor did not hold.'

Then he urged me on with his arguments,
And when silence became worse than speaking;
I said: 'Father, since you have washed away

The sins that I am about to commit,
Such a long promise, fulfilled in so short a time
Will make you triumph in you high seat.'

Saint Francis came for me after I was dead,
But one of the black Cherubim said to him:
'Do not take him; He is mine;

He must come down with my other servants,
Because he gave fraudulent advice
And I have been waiting for his head;

Someone cannot be absolved if they do not repent,
Nor can someone both sin and repent at the same time,
Because one will cancel out the other.'

Oh how I shuddered when he grabbed me
And I cried out: 'Wait, did you think
That I was a looking at the logic of my actions?'

He took me to Minos, who wrapped his tail
Eight times around his stubborn back,
And after that, he bit it in great rage,

And said: 'He goes to burn with the thieves;'
Therefore, I am lost right here where you see me,
Wrapped in flame and carrying resentment and regret."

When the flame had finished speaking,
It moved on, still uttering its lamentations,
Writhing and flapping its sharp-pointed tip.

So we moved on, both me and my Conductor,
Up over the bridge and on to another arch,
Which covers the circle, where penalties are paid by those

Who have sown discord and have thus earned their punishment.

INFERNO: CANTO XXVIII

No one would be able to describe,
In full, the wounds and the blood
That I saw now, no matter how long they tried.

Any description would certainty fall short
Because mere words and even memories,
Would not be able to comprehend so much pain.

If you could bring together all the people
That are now, or ever were in the land
Of Puglia who cried over their wounds and the blood

Shed by the Romans and the lingering war
Over the taking of the great rings,
As Livy has recorded without error,

And mingled those who felt the agony of the blows
Who stood against Robert Guiscard,
Plus all the rest, whose bones are still gathered

At Ceperano, where each man was a traitor,
And those who were at Tagliacozzo,
Where Alardo conquered without weapons,

And added everyone who had been stabbed or lost a limb,
It would be nothing compared
With the disgusting sites of the ninth circle.

A cask of wine, having lost its center support,
Was never shattered as much, as one person I saw
Who was split from his chin to his ass.

His entrails were hanging down between his legs;
His heart was flopping around, as were
His intestines and his bowels.

While I was staring at him,

He looked at me, pulled open his chest
With his hands and said: "See how I can pull myself apart;

See how mutilated I am;
In front of me, another goes weeping as well,
His face is split open from forehead to chin;

And all the others that you see here,
Were ones who spread scandal and divided the people
While they were living, and therefore are split like me.

A devil is behind us, who cruelly slices us
Like this, using the edge of his sword
Slashing us again and again,

Each time we walk down this miserable road;
As we walk, our wounds slowly and painfully close
And then we are split again as we pass him.

But who are you, watching from the bridge,
Maybe you are trying to postpone your own pain
That will be given to you because of how you were judged?"

"Death has not reached him yet,
And guilt does not bring him here to be tortured,"
My Master replied, "But only to allow him the experience,

I, who am dead, have been asked to conduct him
Down here through Hell, from circle to circle;
And this is the truth."

More than a hundred people heard him speak,
And they stooped in the moat to look at me in such wonder
That they were oblivious of their torture.

"Then you should warn Fra Dolcino,
When you return to the place of the sun,

That if he does not want to follow me down here,

That he should stock up on food, or else the snow
Will give the Novarese their victory,
A conquest that will not easily be won otherwise."

He said this to me,
And lifted his foot to leave,
Stepped forward and went on his way.

Another soul, who had his throat pierced through,
And nose cut off close underneath his brow,
And who only had one ear,

Stopped to look in wonder with the others,
Then he stepped forward and pulled open his throat,
Which was red on all sides, and he said:

"You, whose guilt has not condemned you,
And who I once saw up in Italy,
Unless I was deceived by someone who looked like you,

Please speak well of Pier da Medicina,
If ever you see that lovely place again
Where Vercelli slopes down to Marcabo,

And make it known to the best two people of Fano,
Messer Guido and Angiolello,
That if our seeing the future is not in vain,

That they will be tossed over from their ship,
And drowned near Cattolica,
By the betrayal of a fallen tyrant.

Between the isles of Cyprus and Majorca
Neptune has not yet beheld so great a crime,
Neither by pirates nor Argolic people.

That traitor, who has only one eye,
And holds the land, which someone here with me
Wishes he had never set eyes on,

Will make them come to talk to him;
Tell them not to waste their breath or prayers
For they will not escape from Focara's wind."

And I said to him: "Show me and tell me,
If you want me to spread your words,
Who is this person who will deceive them."

Then he laid his hand on the jaw
Of one of his companions, and his mouth
Opened, crying: "This is him, but he cannot speak.

This man, being banished, drowned every doubt
In Caesar by telling him that
Even a man who is prepared will lose if he hesitates."

How bewildered he appeared to me,
With his tongue hanging out of his split windpipe,
This was Curio, who once was so bold in his speaking!

And one, who had lost both of his hands,
Lifted his stumps in the murky air,
So that the blood spilled onto his face,

Cried out: "You should remember Mosca also,
Who once said 'A thing done has ended!'
Which became a dreadful phrase for the Tuscan people."

"Death to you and your entire family,"
I cried; Then he, accumulating woe upon woe,
Departed, like a person sad and crazed.

But I remained to look at the crowd;
And saw something which I would be afraid
Even to talk about, without more proof,

If it were not that I remembered it so well,
Because memory is the good companion which makes a man bold
When he is pure in his heart.

I saw, and still seem to see it,
A body without a head walking in similar fashion
As the others in the mournful herd walked.

And the body held the severed head by the hair,
Hung from his hand as someone would hold a lantern,
And then he looked at us and said:

"Oh my!" It carried its own head so casually,
And it was as if there were two people, a body and a head;
How this could happen, only God can know.

When it came close to the bridge,
It lifted the arm carrying the head high into the air,
To bring it closer to us so it could speak, and it said:

"You, who can still breath, but are watching the dead,
You can see now what our punishment.
Tell me if there is anything worse than this.

And so that you can tell others about me,
Know that I am Bertram de Born, the same person
Who gave evil comfort to the Young King.

I made the father and the son rebellious;
Achitophel not more than Absalom
As David did with his accursed goadings.

Because I split up two people who were united,
I too have been parted from my head!
Leaving me with just the body.

And this is how you see me now."

INFERNO: CANTO XXIX

There were so many people, and their wounds were so
Different that I could not look away,
I could only stare at them and weep;

But Virgil said: "What are you looking at?
Why are your eyes still riveted down there
On those mournful and mutilated spirits?

You did not do that at the other circles;
Maybe you want to stand here and count them, but you should
Know that this circle is two-and-twenty miles around,

And the moon has already set;
Therefore the time that we have left is brief,
And there is more to be seen than what you are seeing now."

I answered him, "If you had known what I was looking for,
Perhaps you would allow a longer stay."
My Guide turned and left, and I followed behind him

Then I added: "In that cavern which held my attention
too Intently, I think a spirit from my family cries there
Mourning the guilt that he earned when he was above."

Then the Master said:
"Do not spend any more time thinking of him;
Put your mind forward, and leave him behind;

I saw him below the little bridge,
Pointing at you, and waving fiercely with his finger.
I heard him being called Geri del Bello.

That was when you were completely absorbed
By the one who formerly ruled Altaforte,
You did not look his way; so he departed."

"My Conductor, his own violent death,
Which has not yet been avenged,"
I said, "By anyone who shares in his shame,

I imagine that it made him disdainful;
Then he went away without speaking to me,
And that has made me pity him all the more."

We continued to speak as we walked
Until we reached the bridge, over the next circle
Which seemed to have more light shining from below.

When we were standing over the last cloister
Of Malebolge, so that they were spread out
Revealing themselves to us,

Their cries pierced me through and through,
As though they were arrows whose tips where barbed,
So that I had to cover my ears with my hands.

If you gathered all of the pain from the hospitals
Of Valdichiana, Maremma and Sardinia,
From July to September,

You would still not find all of the diseases that were
Gathered In this one moat, and such a stench came from
it
From the decaying flesh of the spirits.

We had descended to the furthest bank
From the long bridge, still staying to the left,
And I could suddenly see much clearer

Down to the bottom of the circle, where the servants
Of the high Lord punishes those who were forgers
When they were up on Earth.

I do not think that there was a sadder sight to see
Even in Aegina when the entire population was sick,
(When was the air full of pestilence,

And the animals, down to the little worm,
All fell, and afterwards the ancient people,
As the poets have confirmed,

Were restored again)
That was how it looked in that dark valley
With the spirits languishing in diverse heaps.

Some were on their bellies, and some laying on their backs
And others crawling and shifting their bodies
Along the miserable road.

We walked on without speaking,
Gazing at and listening to the sick
Who did not have strength enough to lift their bodies.

I saw two spirits sitting and leaning against each other,
As two plates lean against each other when they are drying,
And they were covered scabs from their heads to their feet;

I have never seen a honeycomb scraped so roughly
By a stable-boy whose master is waiting,
Or who simply wants to finish quickly,

As these two were scraping themselves with tooth and nails,
For the savage itching of their skin
Which could never be relieved.

And they dragged their nails down along the scabs,
Like a knife scaling a fish,
Or something with tougher scales.

"You, who are scraping yourself"
Began my Leader to one of them,
"And pulling your skin with your fingers,

Tell me if there are any Italians down here;
Speak while your nails continue to scrape
For all eternity."

"We are Italians, who are sitting here before you,
Both of us," One replied while weeping;
"But who are you, that questions us?"

And the Guide said: "I am one who descends
Down with this living man from cliff to cliff,
And I intend to show him Hell."

Then their mutual support was broken,
And each one turned to me and trembled,
Along with others who had heard his words.

The good Master then said to me:
"Ask them whatever you wish."
And I began, since he had told me to:

"So that your memory does not vanish
From the minds of men, in the world above,
But so it may survive for many years,

Tell me who you are, and where you are from;
Do not let your foul and loathsome punishment
Make you afraid to show yourselves to me."

"I was from Arezzo," One of them said,
"And Albert of Siena had me burned;
But what I died for is not what brought me here.

It is true that I said to him, speaking in jest,
That I could fly into the air,
And anyone who had conceit, but little wit,

Would have had me show to him how; and only
Because I did not make him Daedalus,
He had me burned by the one who held him as his son.

But it is in this last circle of the ten,

Which Minos, who cannot error, has me condemned,
For alchemy, which I practiced in the world above"

And to the Poet I said:
"Were there ever a people as vain as the Sienese?
Certainty not the French by far."

Then the other leper, who had heard me, replied:
"Taking out Stricca,
Who knew the art of moderate expenses,

And Niccolo, who knew the luxurious use
Of cloves and discovered before anyone
That such seeds take root in the garden;

And not to mention the group, among whom
Caccia squandered his vineyards and vast woods,
And where the Abbagliato proffered his wit!

So that you know who is supporting you
Against the Sienese, look closely at me,
So that you can recognize my face,

And you will see I am Capocchio's spirit,
Who used alchemy to make false metals;
You must remember, if I know you well,

How skillful an ape of nature I was."

INFERNO: CANTO XXX

In ancient times when Juno was enraged
Against the Thebans because of Semele,
As she had been more than once,

She could drive King Athamas insane.
One Day, when seeing his wife carrying
Their two children in her arms,

He cried: "Spread out the nets, I want to catch that
Lioness and her pups when they pass;"
And then he extended his hands like claws.

He grabbed his first son, who was named Learchus,
Whirled him around, and smashed him on a rock;
And his wife, still holding the other son, drowned
herself;

When fortune toppled
The Trojan's arrogance,
So that the king was crushed along with his kingdom,

Hecuba, the king's wife, sad, disconsolate, and held
captive,
After finding her daughter Plyxena dead,
And seeing her son, Polydorus,

Left unburied on the ocean shore,
Completely lost her senses and barked like a dog,
Since her mind could not handle the extreme anguish;

But not in the furies of Thebes nor of Troy
Was there ever anyone,
Whether goading beasts, or even other human beings,

Who was so cruel as two spirits, pale and naked,
That I saw, who were biting everything, as they ran like
A wild boar does, when it is turned loose from the sty.

One came up to Capocchio, and grabbing him by the throat,
Sank its teeth into his neck, and started dragging him
So that his belly scraped along the rugged road.

And Aretine, who still stood there trembling, said to me:
"That mad spirit is Gianni Schicchi, and he harasses
Everyone like this with his mad ravings and savage attacks."

I said to him, "In hopes that the other one does not sink
his teeth in you, if you don't mind, please
Tell me who it is, before it darts over here."

And he said to me: "That is the ancient ghost
Of the nefarious Myrrha, who became,
Against all natural love, her father's lover.

She began to sin with him,
By pretending to be another person;
Just like that spirit running over there

So that he can gain the heart of a woman,
By pretending to be Buoso Donati,
And making himself look like the other."

And after the two maniacs had passed
Beyond my sight, I turned back
To look at the other evil-born spirits.

I saw one that would have looked exactly like a lute,
If only his groin had been cut off
At the point where his legs joined his hips.

Bloated with dropsy, so that his limbs were too large
As were the other bodily parts, and this made his face
look very small compared to his belly,

He was forced to keep his mouth open
Like someone who is very thirsty, who will lower his chin
And open his jaw wide to catch a drop of water.

"You, who is not being tormented down here,
Why have you come down to this world of woe?"
He said to us, "Look and see

The misery that has befallen me, Master Adamo;
When I was living, I had everything I wanted,
And now, all I want is a drop of water.

The rivers that flowed from the green hills
Of Cassentin descending down into the Arno,
Making their channels cool and wet,

Would flow right in front of me, but in vain;
For thinking of them only makes me drier
Than this disease which strips the flesh from my face.

The harsh justice that chastises me
Also makes me remember the place where
I sinned, which only makes me sigh all the more.

I can still see Romena, where I counterfeited
The currency imprinted with the image of the Baptist,
The crime for which my body was burned above.

But if I could see the horrid soul of Guido,
Or Alessandro, or their brother down here, I would even
Exchange one last look at Branda's fountain for that.

One of them is here already, if the raving
Spirits that are going round have spoken the truth;
But what does it matter to me, with my useless limbs?

If only I were so light, that in
A hundred years, I could move one inch,
I would have already started on the way,

Seeking him out among these squalid people,
Although the circuit is eleven miles around,
And is not less than half a mile across.

It is my own fault that I am here;
But it was they that persuaded me to coin the florins,
Which had three carats of impurity."

And I said to him: "Who are the two poor wretches
That smoke like steam coming from a wet hand in
winter,
Lying there near your right side?"

"I found them here," He replied, "When I fell
Into this chasm, and since then, they have not turned,
Nor do I think they ever will.

One is the woman who falsely accused Joseph,
The other is Sinon, the betraying Greek of Troy;
It is their burning fever that makes them reek."

And one of them, who felt annoyed
At being talked about in such a bad way,
Slammed his fist against his stomach.

It resounded as though it were a drum;
And Master Adamo hit him in the face,
With an arm that was no less hard,

Saying to him: "Although all movement has been taken
From me, for my limbs are very heavy,
I still have one arm I can use if I need to."

And the other answered back: "When you went into the
fire,
Your arm was not so free and ready for action, but you
Seemed to be able to use it when you were making
coins."

And he replied: "What you say now is true;
But you were not such a true witness back then,
Where you were questioned about the truth at Troy."

"I may have spoken falsely, but you falsified the coin,"
Said Sinon; "And I am here for my one false action,

But you are here for more reasons than any other demon."

"Remember, perjurer, about the horse," he screamed back, "And the whole world knows how horrible it was."
"Not as horrible as the thirst

Which cracks your tongue,"
The Greek said, "And the putrid water
That gives you such a bloated stomach."

Then the false-coiner said:
"It is not as bloated as your gaping mouth;
Because even if I were thirsty and stuffed,

You are the one who is burning and whose head aches,
And it would not take many words to coax you
To lick up the mirror of Narcissus."

I was intently listening to them argue, when the Master
Said to me: "If you insist on staying and watching them,
Then you and I are going to have a fight."
When I heard the anger in his voice,
I turned around to him in shame,
So much so that it still swirls through my memory.

And like someone who dreams of his own harm,
Who, while dreaming, wishes it were just a dream,
And so craves what is, as if it were not;

That is how I became, not having any power to speak,
I wanted to beg for his forgiveness,
And I did, but did not think I did.

"Having less shame can wash away a greater fault,"
The Master said, "Much greater than you just had;
Therefore get rid of your sadness,

And know that I am still here with you, if ever it comes
To pass that fortune brings you to where there are people
who are fighting like this, remember,

It is a weakness to enjoy hearing this kind of bickering."

INFERNO: CANTO XXXI

His quick tongue first wounded me,
So that it made me blush with shame,
And then it comforted me;

I heard that the same was true with Achilles' spear,
Which he got from his father, it was used to first cause
The pain but could also be used to ease the pain.

We turned our backs on the wretched valley,
And climbed the banks surrounding it,
Without saying a word to each other.

Here, it was not quite night, but not quite day either,
So that I could not see very far ahead of me;
But I could hear the blast of a loud horn,

It was so loud it would have made thunder sound faint,
And it made me look, not where I was going,
But rather, I was staring off toward the sound.

After the miserable defeat
When Charlemagne lost all of his holy soldiers,
The sound of Roland's horn was not even this loud.

While I was still looking off to the side,
I thought I saw many high towers standing there,
And I asked: "Master, what city is this?"

And he said to me: "Because what you are looking at
In the darkness is a long way off,
Your mind is playing tricks on you.

You will see when you finally arrive,
How much you have been deceived by the distance;
So, walk a little faster so that we will get there sooner."

Then tenderly he took me by the hand,
And said: "Before we go too much further,

So that you will understand what you are about to see

I want you to know that these are not towers, but giants,
And they are standing in the well, along this bank.
They are hidden from view from their waist down."

As the fog was beginning to fade away,
Little by little the view became clearer
As the mist which filled the air began to disappear,

So, as I looked through the dense and dark air,
Getting closer and closer to the well,
I realized my initial mistake, and became frightened;

As Montereggione crowns itself with towers,
Along its circular walls,
All along the bank which surrounds the well

With one half of their bodies visible
The horrible giants stood, whom Jove torments
Even now from out the heavens.

I could already see the face of one of them,
Shoulders, and chest, and a large part of the belly,
And he held both of his arms down along his sides.

Certainly Nature was wise, when she stopped making
Animals like these,
So that Mars would not have more of them for his army;

And as she has no regrets from making elephants and
whales
Whoever was looking at these giants
Would have to consider it good that she stopped;

For when the mind and intellect
Are added to evil spirit and great power,
No one can make a wall strong enough to stop it.

His face appeared to me as long and large
As the pine-cone at Saint Peter's Basilica in Rome,

And the other parts were in the same proportion;

So that the edge of the bank, which looked like an apron
Hanging down his middle, showed so much of him
Above it, that to reach up to his hair

Three men, standing on each other, would still fail;
And I could see that there was still half of him hidden
Down below his belt line, in the well.

"Raphael mai amech izabi almi,"
He began to clamor from his ferocious mouth,
From which sweet words would never issue forth.

And to him my Guide said: "You idiotic soul,
Keep your horn close at hand, and vent yourself with it,
When wrath or some other passion overcomes you.

Look around your neck, and you will find the belt
Which keeps it fastened, you bewildered soul,
There, hanging across your chest." Then he said to me:

"He blames himself for his wrong doing;
This one is Nimrod, and it is because of his evil deeds
That the world speaks in different languages instead of one.

We will leave him and not bother talking to him;
Because, he cannot understand any language he hears,
As his language cannot be understood by others."

Therefore we continued our journey,
Turned to the left, and it was a long time before
We found another giant far more fierce and large.

Whoever was strong enough to bind him,
I cannot say; but he was held tight
With his right arm behind, and his left arm in front,

With chains, that were wrapped around him
From the neck down, covering the part I could see,

It wound itself around at least five times.

"This proud one wanted to test
His own power against the Supreme God, Jove,"
My Leader said, "And this was his reward.

His name is Ephialtes; And he showed great power
When the giants terrified the gods;
But the arms he used back then, he will never move again."

And I said to him: "If it is possible, I would like to see
The massive body of Briareus
Since I will never have this opportunity again."

And he replied: "You will see Antaeus
Very soon, who can speak and is not tied up,
And he will take us to the very bottom of Hell.

Later on, you will have the chance to see the one you want,
And he is bound, and fastened like this one,
Except that he seems to be more ferocious."

There never was an earthquake that was so strong
That it could shake a tower so violently,
As Ephialtes suddenly shook himself.

Then I was more afraid of death than ever,
And fear alone might have killed me,
If I had not seen the manacles that held him.

Then we continued to walk on, and came to Antaeus,
Who was amazingly tall, and would have been, even if
You did not count his head, as his body emerged from the cavern.

"You, who are from the great valley,
Which Scipio made glorious,
When he turned back Hannibal with his entire army,

You, who once captured a thousand lions,
And who was at the mighty war
With your brothers, who some still think

That you would have been victorious:
If you would please place us down below,
There where the cold keeps Cocytus locked up.

Do not make us go to Tityus nor Typhoeus;
Since you can give us what we ask for;
Therefore, please stoop down and scoop us up.

When this one returns to the world, he will restore your fame;
Because he still lives, and expects to have a long life,
If Grace does not call him too soon."

The Master said; and quickly, the giant
Extended his hands and took up my Guide,--
Hands whose great pressure Hercules once felt.

Virgil, when he felt himself embraced,
Said to me: "Stay close to me, and I'll carry you;"
Then he pulled me close to his chest.

As the leaning side of the Carisenda must look
From below, when a cloud goes above it
So that it hangs on the opposite side;

This is how Antaeus seemed to me,
When I saw him stoop down, and it was then that
I wished we could go to the bottom some other way.

But he put us down lightly in the abyss,
Which swallows both Judas and Lucifer;
Once he put us down, he immediately stood back up,

Tall and straight, as a mast rises upward on a ship.

INFERNO: CANTO XXXII

If I ever thought of words that were rough and crude
Enough to describe this dismal hole
Which held the weight of the rest of Hell,

I would squeeze them from my brain;
But, because I could not possibly define it completely,
I find it difficult to begin at all;

It is not something to be taken lightly;
You cannot use small words or baby talk when
Describing the bottom of the entire universe.

Hopefully, those Heavenly Ladies can help me find the words,
As they helped Amphion in surrounding Thebes,
That can make you fully comprehend what I saw.

Down here are the worst of the ill-begotten rabble,
Residing in a place that is so harsh, that their lives would
Have been better for them if they were sheep or goats!

We continued down into the deep, dark well,
Beneath the giant's feet, but lower down.
I was scanning the high walls around us

When I heard someone say to me: "Watch where you are stepping!
Be careful not to trample
The heads of the tired, miserable brothers!"

I quickly looked around and saw that I was standing
On a lake that, because of the frost,
Looked like glass instead of water.

There was never a veil of ice this thick,
Even in winter on the Danube in Austria,
Nor beneath the frigid sky of the Don,

As there was here on this lake; so that if Tambernich
Had fallen on it, or Pietrapana,
Even at the edge, it would not have made even a creak.

And as a frog, in order to croak, places himself
With his muzzle out of water near harvest time,
When the peasant-girls sit dreaming,

So these miserable souls sank into the ice,
Buried up to their necks,
With their teeth chattering loudly.

Each one of them had his head bent down;
Their mouths resounded with the depths of the coldness,
But their eyes portrayed the sadness in their hearts.

I looked around, trying to take in the scene before me,
And then I looked down and saw two souls so close,
That the hair on their heads was mingled together.
"You two, who are pressed so close together,"
I said, "Who are you?" They bent their heads towards me
And when they had lifted up their faces,

Their eyes, which at first were only moist,
Suddenly gushed over, and the frost congealed
Their tears between them, and locked them up again.

A clamp never bound together two pieces of wood
So tightly; and then they, like two goats,
Butted their heads together, as their wrath overcame
them.

And another soul, who had lost his ears because of the
cold,
With his head still facing down said to me:
"Why do you stand there looking at us?

If you want to know who these two are,
The valley where the Bisenzio descends
Belonged to them and to their father Albert.

They came from one body, and if you search through
All of Caina, you will not find a soul
More worthy to be fixed in this ice;

Not he whose body and spirit were taken
In a single blow by Arthur's hand;
Not Focaccia; not this one here who blocks my view

With his head so that I can't see in front of me,
Who bore the name of Sassol Mascheroni;
You know who he was, if you are indeed a Tuscan.

And to save you from asking me,
I will tell you that I was Camicion de' Pazzi,
And I wait for Carlino to exonerate me."

Then I saw a thousand faces, made
Purple with cold and it suddenly made me shudder,
Which I still do when I come upon a frozen pond.

And while we were moving towards the middle,
Where everything converges together,
I was shivering in the eternal darkness.

Whether it was will, or destiny, or chance,
I do not know; but in walking among the heads
I struck one of them in the face with my foot.

Weeping he growled at me: "Why do you trample on me?
Unless you have come to increase the vengeance
Of Montaperti, why did you kick me?"

And I said: "Master, please wait here for me,
I need to clear something up with this one;
Then I will go as fast as you want me to."

The Leader stopped; and I said to the one
Who was still blaspheming vehemently:
"Who are you, that you feel you must insult others?"

And he replied, "Who are you that goes through
Antenora kicking
Other people's heads? If you were living
Would you have kicked me so hard?"

"I am living" was my response,
"And if you want me to spread your fame,
You would do well to give me your name for my notes."

And he said to me: "Fame is the last thing I would want;
Get out of here, and don't give me any more trouble;
You obviously don't know how to flatter someone down
here."

Then I seized him by the scalp, and said:
"Tell me your name, or I will rip out your hair."
Then he said to me:

"Go ahead and rip out my hair,
I will not tell you who I am, nor show you my face,
Even if you kicked my head a thousand times."

I had his hair already twisted in my hand,
And I pulled out a patch of it.
He screamed but held his eyes firmly downward,

When another spirit cried: "What is bothering you now,
Bocca?
Isn't it enough to clatter with your teeth,
So now you decide to scream? What devil has overcome
you?"

"Now," I said, "I don't care if you speak or not,
You accursed traitor; for I will report your shame
When I spread the news of finding you here."

"Begone," he screamed, "And say whatever you want to,
But when you are spreading your news, don't be silent
About the one who just spoke to you;

He weeps here from the silver he got from the French;

You can tell everyone that the one from Duera
Is punished here where the traitors are stuck in the ice.

If you want to know who else is here,
The one beside you is the traitor of Beccaria,
Who lost his head in Florence;

Gianni del Soldanier, I think, may be
Over there with Ganellon, and Tebaldello
Who opened Faenza to their enemies when the people slept."

I left him, and joined my guide. As we walked
I saw two spirits frozen in one hole,
So that one head was a hood for the other;

And as bread is devoured through hunger,
The uppermost one had his teeth sunk into the neck
Of the other where the brain is connected to the back.

In the same way that Tydeus gnawed
On the temples of Menalippus in disdain,
This one gnawed on the skull of the other.

"You, who are acting like a beast and showing
Your hatred against him who you are eating,
Tell me why you are doing this," I said,

"And I will promise you, that if you have a rightful complaint Against him, by knowing who you are, and his transgression,
When I return to the world above, I will repay you,

For as long as I am still able to speak."

INFERNO: CANTO XXXIII

The sinner lifted up his mouth,
And wiped it on the hair of the same head that he had been Chewing on. Then he began:

"You want me to tell you of the desperate grief
That tears at my heart just to think of it,
Much less speak of it;

But if my words will bring
Infamy to the traitor that I am gnawing on,
I will speak to you, and weep the entire time.

I don't know who you are,
Nor how you got here; but you seem like a Florentine
Especially when I hear you speak.

You should know that I was Count Ugolino,
And this one was Ruggieri the Archbishop;
Now I will tell you why I am here with him.

I trusted him, but because of his malicious deeds,
I was put into prison,
And afterwards put to death, but you know that;

Nevertheless what you do not know, is just how cruel
that Death really was, but I will tell you,
And you will see how heartless he was to me.

Through a narrow window in my prison tower, which was called
The Tower of Famine because of what happened to me,
And in which others must still be locked up,

I watched many moons go by
Until I dreamed the evil dream
Which finally showed me the future.

This person here appeared to me as lord and master,

Hunting a wolf and its pups on the mountain
Which blocks Lucca from seeing the Pisans.

With hunting dogs, gaunt, and eager, and well trained,
He sent out Gualandi with Sismondi and Lanfianchi
Ahead of him.

After a brief run, the father and sons grew tired,
And then the sharp fangs were upon them, and
It seemed to me that I saw their legs ripped open.

When I finally woke up, before sunrise,
I heard my sons moaning in their sleep
As they lay near me, and asking for bread.

You are indeed cruel, if you do not grieve,
Knowing what I felt in my heart when I heard their pleas,
And if that does not make you cry, then nothing can.

They woke up, and it was almost the time
When our food would normally be brought to us,
But because of this dream, we were all apprehensive;

Then I heard the lower door of the tower close and lock
And without speaking a word
I gazed into the faces of my sons.

I did not cry, and inside, I turned to stone;
They wept; and my darling little Anselm said:
'You do not look good, father, what is bothering you?'

Still I did not shed a tear, nor answer him
For the rest of that day, nor the following night,
Until the next morning.

Then the first ray of sunlight shone
In that miserable prison, and I saw
My own face on the four faces of my sons,

I bit both of my hands in agony;
And, they thought that it was because I was hungry

Since they had just woken up, and one of them said

'Father, we would be in less pain if you would eat us.
You were the one who clothed us with this poor skin,
And you should be the one to strip it off.'

I calmed down then, so that they would not be sad.
That day we were all silent, and the next day as well.
Ah! Unmerciful earth, why didn't you open up and
swallow us?

When we had come unto the fourth day, Gaddo
Threw himself down outstretched at my feet,
Saying, 'Father, why didn't you help me?'

And there he died; and, as you see me now,
I saw the three of them fall, one by one, between
The fifth day and the sixth;

I was already blind, and began to feel for them.
For three days I called to them after they were dead;
Then hunger made me do what sorrow could not."

After he said this, his eyes flared with rage.
He sank his teeth into the skull in front of him,
And tore at the bone like a dog.

Ah! Pisa, there is so much shame on the people
Of your fair land who, always seem to say 'Yes' to
everything.
Since your neighbors are slow to punish you,

Let the Capraia and Gorgona move,
And make a dam across the mouth of the Arno
So that every person in your city may drown!

For if Count Ugolino was accused
Of having betrayed you within your walls,
You still should not have punished his sons.

They were guiltless of any crime, you modern Thebes!

Their youth made them innocent. Uguccione and
Brigata,
And the other two named before!

We continued on to where the rugged ice
Held another group of people trapped. This group was
Not looking down, but all of them were looking up.

The act of weeping itself stopped them from weeping,
And the grief that could not be released from their eyes
Turned itself inward to increase their anguish;

Because when the first tears begin to form,
They freeze like a crystal visor,
Filling the entire cup beneath the eyebrow.

Just like a hard callus of skin,
Because of the cold, I had lost all sensation
And could not feel anything in my face,

Still it seemed to me as though I felt some wind;
And I said: "Master, where is that wind coming from?
Is not all motion in the air stopped this far down?"

And he said to me: "Soon enough, you will see with your
own eyes
Where this is coming from,
And what is causing this blast of air."

One of the wretches trapped in the frozen crust
Cried out to us: "You merciless souls
Who have been cast down to this final pit of Hell,

Break these rigid veils from my eyes, so that I
Can vent the sorrow which strangles my heart,
At least a little, before my tears freeze again."

And I said to him: "If you want me to help you
Tell me who you were; and then, if I don't free you,
May I go to the bottom of the ice."

Then he replied: "I am Friar Alberigo;
I was the one who offered the fruits of the evil garden,
And down here, I am given dates for the figs I gave above."

I said to him, "Wait. Are you already dead?"
And he said to me:
"I do not know how my body is doing in the upper world.

Many times, the soul ends up here
Before Atropos has arrived to take it.
This can happen here in Ptolomaea.

And, so that you are more willing to remove
These glassy tears from my eyes, I will tell you that
As soon as any soul betrays another, as I have done,

His body is taken over by a demon,
Who rules it from that point on,
For as long as it remains alive.

The person's soul rushes down into this frozen Hell;
This is true also for the person that is behind me,
His body may still be up in the world above as well.

You should know this, since you have just come down;
It is Ser Branca d' Oria, and many years
Have passed away since he was locked down here."

I said to him, "I think that you are trying to deceive me;
For Branca d' Oria is not dead yet.
He eats, and drinks, and sleeps, and puts on clothes."

"In the moat of the Malebranche above," he said,
"There are pools of boiling pitch,
And Michel Zanche had not yet arrived there,

When this one behind me left a devil
In his own body as well as some of his family,
And together they made the betrayal.

Now, stretch out your hand,
And open my eyes;" But I didn't,
Being rude to him was actually a courtesy.

Ah, Genoese! Your men are always at odds
With every virtue and full of every vice.
Why have they not been purged from the world?

For with the vilest spirit of Romagna
I have found one of you, who, for his deeds,
His soul already bathes in Cocytus,

And still his body remains alive!

INFERNO: CANTO XXXIV

"'Vexilla Regis prodeunt Inferni'
The king of Hell is in front of us,"
My Master said, "See if you can find him."

Like the air, when it is filled with a heavy fog,
Or when the light of day is fading into night,
And a windmill is turning slowly in the distance,

I thought I saw a building like this ahead of us;
And, to protect myself from the wind, I slid behind
My Guide, because there was no place else to hide.

There I was, and I still shake even as I write it,
With the souls buried in the ice,
Each of them looking like straws stuck into glass.

Some were lying down, others were standing erect,
Some showing their heads, and others only showing
their feet;
Another, was bent over, his head bowed down to his feet.

After we had walked a little further,
My Master was happy to point out to me
The creature who had once been beautiful,

He came to a stop and said to me:
"This is the place known as Dis, And it is here
That you must show more courage than ever before."

Suddenly, I became frozen and powerless.
Don't ask me why, I would not be able to explain it,
Because language does not have words that would be
sufficient.

I did not die, but nor was I alive;
Think for yourself, if you can imagine it,
What I became, being deprived of both life and death.

The Emperor of this miserable kingdom
From the middle of his chest downward was buried in ice;
And I would be closer to the height of a giant

Than a giant would be if compared to the length of his arms;
Just think of how huge his entire body must be,
If his arms alone are longer than a giant is tall.

Where he was once beautiful, he had become equally ugly,
And he lifted up his face towards the Heavens,
Which poured down the misery and grief on him.

Then, I saw, to my great surprise,
That he had three faces on his head!
The one in front was bright red in color;

The two other faces were joined with the first
Above the middle part of each shoulder,
And they were all joined together at the top of the head;

The right one was a mixture of white and yellow;
The left one was dark brown, similar in color to the people
Who come from where the Nile falls to the valley.

Underneath each head, there were two mighty wings,
As huge as you would expect from such a giant a bird;
I have never seen sails of a ship that were this large.

The wings did not have feathers, but were more like a bat,
And he was flapping them,
So that three winds were produced from them.

This was how Cocytus remained completely frozen.
With all six eyes he wept, and down all three chins
Trickled the tear-drops and his bloody drool.

In each mouth his teeth were crunching
A sinner, grinding and chewing on him,
So that he could torture three of them at the same time.

To the one in front, the biting was nothing compared
To the clawing that was being done, and sometimes the spine
Would be completely stripped of skin.

"That soul up there that is suffering the most,"
The Master said, "Is Judas Iscariot;
With his head inside, he kicks his legs on the outside.

The other two, whose heads are out,
The one who hangs from the dark mouth is Brutus;
See how he writhes, but does not speak.

And the other, who still looks strong, is Cassius.
But night is almost here and it is time
For us to leave, because we have seen everything."

He motioned to me and I clasped him around the neck.
He watched intently for a good opportunity,
And when the wings were spread wide apart,

He grabbed hold of Lucifer's shaggy sides;
Pulling hand over hand, we descended down along his body
Between the thick hair and the frozen crust.

When we came to where the thigh connects to the hip
Right where the joint is located,
My Guide, while pulling hard, and short of breath,

Turned his head and looked back the way we had come.
Then he pulled the hair, and began to climb,
So that I thought we were returning to Hell.

"Hold on tight,"
The Master said, panting as though he were fatigued,
"This is the only way we can get out."

We climbed through an opening in the rocks,
And he set me down on the ledge;
Then he climbed up and joined me there.

I looked up and expected to see
Lucifer the same way I had left him;
Instead, I saw him from below, kicking his legs.

If I seem confused,
Then it is only because I didn't understand
What exactly I went through on this climb.

"Get up on your feet," the Master said,
We have a long and difficult road ahead of us,
And the sun is now high in the sky."

This was no palace corridor that we were standing in
But more like some rocky dungeon,
With an uneven floor and almost no light.

"Master, before we are out of this abyss,"
I said when I stood up,
"Can you please explain something to me;

Where is the ice? And how is Lucifer suddenly
Upside down? And how did the time go from night
To day so quickly, in just moments?"

And he said to me: "You still think that you are
Near the center of the Earth, where I grabbed
The hair of Lucifer and started our descent.

And we were, for as long as I was descending; But when
You thought I had turned around, what happened was that
We passed through the center, so everything was reversed,

And we have now come to the opposite hemisphere
On the other side, away from dry land and

Are now below the area where they sacrificed Jesus,

The man who was born and lived without sin.
You are now standing on the side of the planet
In which Judecca was formed.

Here it is morning when it is evening on the other side;
And Lucifer, who's hair we used as our stairway,
Is still fixed in the ice, and has not moved.

This is where he fell down out of heaven;
And the land that was on this side was forced to the other,
And he was covered by the sea.

All the land was moved to our hemisphere,
So what you see on this side
Is the vacant space that was left behind.

This place down here, away from Lucifer,
Reaching as far as his tomb extends,
Is not known by sight, but instead, by the sound

Of a small stream. It descends down here
Through a chasm within the stone, which it has gnawed
Away over time, and that winds around and gently falls."
The Guide and I walked along that hidden road
To return to the bright world outside;
And without stopping to rest

We climbed up, him first and me following,
Until I saw through a small, round opening
Some of the beautiful things that Heaven holds;

Then we climbed out and looked up at the stars.

THE END

Made in the USA
Lexington, KY
31 August 2015